NIGHT
FLIGHTS

PHILIP REEVE

NIGHT FLIGHTS

ILLUSTRATED BY IAN McQUE

SCHOLASTIC INC.

First published in the United Kingdom in 2018 by Scholastic UK Ltd., Euston House, 24 Eversholt Street, London NW1 1DB.

ISBN 978-1-338-28970-1

10 9 8 7 6 5 4 3 2 1   18 19 20 21 22

Printed in the U.S.A.   40
First printing 2018

Book design by Jamie Gregory. This edition adapted by Christopher Stengel.

*To Jihae, who plays Anna Fang with such style and
grace that I realized she needed some more stories*

CONTENTS

Airhaven hung on the evening wind. The huge gasbags of the flying town were touched with golden light like sunset clouds, but the land below it was already in shadow, except where water reflected the sky in the flooded track-marks that scarred the plains and hills. Here and there, a cluster of moving lights showed where a town or a small traction city was making its way through the deepening twilight. A slow, old trading town was moving south through a gap in the mountains, and a pack of predator villages was milling after it, waiting for their chance to attack. It was hunt or be hunted down there.

But no one in Airhaven had to worry about such things. Nothing hunted Airhaven, where aviators and air-traders from the Traction Cities mingled on almost-friendly terms with flyers from the static strongholds of the Anti-Traction League. In the low-roofed, lamp-lit public rooms of the Gasbag and Gondola, Airhaven's finest pub, traders from London did deals with merchants from Lahore, and travelers from the Traktiongrads learned the latest songs from Nuevo Maya. There was good food and good drink, and soft beds for aviators who wanted a change from the narrow bunks aboard their airships. And best of all, there were stories to be heard, for no one had such good stories as the men and women who made their lives upon the Bird Roads, and no one took such pleasure in the telling of them.

That night, a large group had gathered around the circular table in the main bar, under one of the propellers from the old air-clipper Tardigrade, which had been repurposed as a ceiling fan. Nils Lindstrom was there, the captain of the freighter Garden Aeroplane Trap; he had been making everyone's flesh creep with an account of unearthly things he had seen in the Ice Wastes. Now Yasmina Rashid of the privateer Zainab was telling of a running fight she'd had with pirate box kites above the dry, red hills of Yemen, while Jean-Claude Reynault of the La Belle Aurore chipped in with his tale of a similar battle over the Yellow Sea. Coma Korzienowski, commander of Traktionstadt Coblenz's armed reconnaissance vessel Todeswurst, listened with a look on her face that let the others know she had a story of her own to tell, and that it was going to be a good one.

"So what about you, Anna Fang?" asked Reynault, when Yasmina had finished with her pirates. "You've flown farther than any of us. Don't you have a tale to share?"

The woman he was speaking to sat on the far side of the table. She had tipped her chair back so it leaned against the wall, and her face was in shadow. A handsome, wind-browned woman with streaks of white in her short black hair. She had listened to all the stories that evening and laughed as loud as anyone at the funny parts, but she had said nothing, and she said nothing now, just smiled at Reynault. Her teeth were stained red with the juice of betel nuts.

"Anna doesn't tell her stories," said Yasmina. "Short answers to long questions, that's her way. She'll tell you, 'I grew up in the slave-holds of Arkangel and built my airship out of parts I stole,' but she'll never tell you how or when."

"Or she'll say, 'I flew over the haunted deserts of America once,'" said Lindstrom, "but she'll never tell you what she saw there. People tell stories about Anna, but Anna never tells them herself."

"She's a spy for the Anti-Traction League," said Coma Korzienowski. "She's been trained to tell no one anything, and when she does tell you something it's most likely a lie. Isn't that right, Anna?"

Anna Fang laughed. "Let's hear Coma's story," she said. "She's been itching to tell it all night."

Coma protested that she had not, then started telling it anyway. It was a story that Anna had heard before, so she did not bother following the words, just let herself enjoy the sound of Coma's voice, the laughter of the others, their faces in the lamplight. She was fond of them all; some were old friends and some old adversaries, and here in Airhaven the difference did not matter much. But she did not want to share her stories with them. Stories changed when you told them. You made up new details to please your listeners, you exaggerated things or left things out, and soon even you came to believe the new story was the real one. Anna wanted hers to stay the same, as true as her memory could keep them.

But perhaps she should tell someone, she thought. Perhaps when she next flew home to Shan Guo she would tell Sathya, the barefoot kid she'd rescued down in Kerala, who was the closest thing that Anna had to family. She would start at the beginning, with the one story about Anna Fang that everybody knew, of how she had escaped from the slave-pens of Arkangel when she was just a girl, in an airship she had built for herself.

Except that the real story had been, like all real things, more complicated than stories made it sound . . .

FROZEN
HEART

Anna knew what they were as soon as she saw them. Twin Jeunet-Carot engine-pods, all the way from Paris. Her parents' ship had been powered by pods like those. Anna's father had always said they were the best aero-engines ever built. They had carried the Aerial Merchant Vessel *Mermaid* uncomplainingly along the Bird Roads for the whole of Anna's childhood, and it had not been the pods' fault when the wind changed unexpectedly above the Tannhäuser Mountains one day and they were choked with the fine ash from a volcano.

Even then, they could have been fixed. Anna's parents had steered the ship safely down onto a little traction town with a good air-harbor and set to work, but before they could finish the repairs, a storm swept down on the town, and in the heart of the storm came Arkangel, the Hammer of the High Ice, the greatest predator city of the north.

Anna had caught one dreadful glimpse into the city's furnace-lined gut as its huge jaws hinged open. When they slammed shut upon the helpless town, the part of it where Anna and her parents were cowering had buckled and her mother had lost her grip on Anna's hand and tumbled through a gap that opened suddenly between two deckplates, down into the oily workings of the town's massive caterpillar tracks. The tracks had been moving at full speed and had crushed Anna's mother in an instant, but they could not pull the town free of Arkangel's jaws, and it had been dragged backward into the city's gut amid a cacophony of machinery and stressed metal. It was so loud that Anna had not even been able to hear her own screams as Arkangel's soldiers separated her from her father and dragged them off to join the other slaves.

Ever since, she had lived in Arkangel's belly while it skated endlessly across the ice sheets on its huge runners. She had lost everything—even her name had been replaced with a number: K-420. She had become one of the countless thralls who serviced the dismantling machines and the huge engines. (*Thralls* was what they

called their slaves in Arkangel. Anna supposed the people who lived on the city's warm and comfortable upper tiers thought it sounded nicer.)

And now Arkangel had eaten yet another town, and Anna's work-gang had been detailed to sort through the mounds of salvage that had been thrown off it so that the giant saws and cutting torches and mechanical pincers could start ripping its upperworks apart.

It was in one of those mounds that Anna found the engines. There was a lot of old machinery there, probably the contents of some air-chandler's store. Most of it was junk, and the two engine-pods lay side by side among it, rusty and dusty and missing their propellers, so that anyone who hadn't lived aboard an airship might not have known what they were at all. But Anna knew. She wiped the grime off a brass plaque with the cuff of her coveralls and there was the makers' logo, the curly-tailed dragon she had liked so much when she was little.

It was confusing to have such a vivid memory of her childhood called up so suddenly and so clearly. Mostly Anna tried not to remember those times. It wasn't because the memories were bad ones; it was because they were good. She had been happy in the sky with Ma and Pa, and she knew that if she thought about that time too often, it would make her so sad that she would die.

People died often in the thrall yards; from accidents,

from illness, or just worn out by endless work. Thralls were allowed few comforts and precious little food, especially in deep winter when prey was scarce. Anna's father had been assigned to a different part of the Gut, but for the first few months he kept finding ways to visit Anna and slip a little extra food to her. Each time he looked thinner. At first he would tell her that they would find a way out, but she soon realized that he did not believe that, and before long he stopped bothering to say it. His eyes, which had been twinkly and full of fun and love for her when she lived in the sky, turned as dull as the windows of an empty house. One day he did not come at all, and after a week without seeing him Anna asked her overseer what had become of him and the overseer talked with an overseer from Pa's work-gang and then told her with a small shrug, "Dead."

The overseer's name was Verna Mould. She was a hard woman, but she was not unkind (it was she who had allowed Anna's father to visit, and asked only a small part of the extra rations in return). Seeing Anna's mouth start to tremble as the bad news sank in, she added helpfully, "He's as dead as you'll be, girly, if you waste your time in grieving. If you want to survive down here, you got to stop caring about anyone but yourself. You start fretting about others, or moping and mourning and thinking about old times, you'll waste away and die like he did, or get careless and stand in the way of a salvage grab, or fall into a smelter. Forget all that stuff and you can thrive down here. You might end up being made an overseer yourself one day. That's the best life a thrall can hope for aboard the Hammer."

So Anna had tried to forget everything, or at least to bundle her memories up and stuff them away in some dark room deep inside herself. But now she was running the tips of her fingers over the cute little embossed dragons on a pair of Jeunet-Carot engine-pods, just as she had as a little girl, and it was as if a key had come to unlock that room and let the cold, clear sunlight of long ago shine in painfully on everything.

She wiped her eyes on the sleeve of her greasy coveralls and tried to think straight. There were rewards for thralls who found valuable pieces of salvage. There would be extra rations of food, and Verna Mould would let Anna keep some of it for herself. Even so, she still hesitated for a moment before she let anyone know of her discovery. She felt that the aviator whose ship these engines came from must have been proud of them once and would think it a shame that they had ended up here in the belly of Arkangel.

But she knew that if she didn't claim the bonus, one of her comrades would, so she turned and shouted, "Here! Here! Salvage! Two old aero-engines, might still be good for parts . . ."

That night, in her metal bunk in the thrall-hold, Anna was shaken out of her uneasy dreams by Verna Mould. "Wake up, K-420!" the overseer ordered. "The bosses want to see you! It is about those engines that you found!"

She rolled off her bunk and went blearily after the older woman through Arkangel's Gut. Massive circular saws were biting into the chassis of the captured town, making trees of sparks whose tops brushed the Gut's steel roof. Above that roof was the rest of Arkangel, the warm Core where the bosses lived. Anna had never been up there, never thought about it much. She knew she worked for a company called Kael Industries, and she knew it was run by a man called Viktor Kael because his ugly old face was on posters in the thrall-holds. His white beard and chilly eyes made him look like an ice-giant in a story. Was he the one who wanted to talk to her? Anna shivered.

At the edge of the salvage yards were big freight elevators; metal cages inside metal cages. Anna stepped into one. Verna Mould closed it behind her and said, "Good luck, K-420." She watched as the cage went rattling up into the drifts of fumes that hung beneath the roof. Then she shrugged, and turned away, and carefully put K-420's frightened, sleepy face out of her mind as she trudged back to her own bunk. She had known other thralls who had been summoned up top, and none of them had ever been seen again.

When the elevator reached the next level, Anna found two Kael Industries security men waiting for her. They beckoned her out of the elevator cage and went with her along a corridor to a doorway, which they said she should go through. It led into a scruffy little room where an electric lamp swung from the low ceiling. There was a desk with two chairs. The chair on Anna's side of the desk was empty. In the other, facing her, sat a young man. He wasn't much to look at, with his wan, bony face and limp red hair, but he was wearing fur-lined silk and rings on his fingers and a look that let Anna know he was from one of Arkangel's ruling families.

"You are the thrall K-420? The girl who found those Jeunet-Carots?" he asked, pushing aside a notebook in which he had been scribbling. He smiled. "Please, take a seat."

No one had said please to Anna since the day she first became a thrall. No one smiled at thralls. No one ever offered them a seat. She glanced behind her, suspecting a trick. But the door she had come through had been closed, and the security men were on the other side of it, and the young man said again, "Sit down. Please."

Warily, Anna settled herself on the seat he kept pointing at. She saw his face twist in dismay as the stench of her filthy coveralls and unwashed body crept across the desk and up his nostrils. "Great gods," he muttered, and then, recovering, "It is about those engines . . ."

"I didn't mean no harm," said Anna, who still assumed that she had done something wrong. "I thought there was still some use in them, if only as parts."

"Oh, there is! There is!" said the young man. "What interests me is how you *knew* that. Not many people would. Not many . . . people of your class, I mean."

"I was in the air-trade," Anna said. "My parents were, when I was growing up. Before I was caught."

"I see! And your parents are . . . ?"

"Dead," said Anna, with a little shrug.

The young man made a noise that he probably thought sounded sympathetic. He stuck out a clean white hand for Anna to shake, then thought better of it and just smiled at her some more. He wanted her to like him, she realized. How weak would someone have to be to need a thrall's approval?

"I'm Stilton Kael," he said. "I'm Viktor Kael's youngest son. I'm working on a private project, sort of a hobby, really; my father doesn't exactly approve, but he's agreed I can transfer one thrall from general duties to help me. I'm looking for one who knows about airships."

He turned the notebook around and slid it across the desk to Anna. The pages were so white that she was afraid to touch them with her grimy fingers. Stilton Kael turned them for her, as if he was eager for her to see the spidery black writing he had covered them with. Writing and numbers and diagrams. Anna realized that she was looking at the plans for an airship.

"The Boreal Regatta is setting off from Arkangel this coming summer," he said. "It's the greatest air-race in the Northern Hemisphere. Two thousand miles, right over the pole, to the finishing point, where the city of Anchorage will be waiting. 'High above Earth's icy crown / those daring flyers seek renown!' That's how I describe it in a poem I'm writing. But I am not just a poet, K-420! I mean to enter the Boreal Regatta, and I mean to win it! I am building my own ship. I have some ideas about aerodynamics, you see. I've gathered quite a few bits for her these past six months—the airframe from a Helsinki warship, a silicon-silk envelope, reinforced gas-cells—it's amazing what you can find in the scrapyards. Those engines you spotted today are just what I need to power her. Come on! I'll show you!"

So she followed Stilton Kael through metal corridors, past the warehouses where Kael Industries stored their salvage and the workshops where they repaired it, or rebuilt it into new things to sell to the people of the city. He led her to a door near the outer hull, one of many stenciled with the Kael logo. His pallid fingers skittered over the keypad of an old-tech lock. The door opened, and Anna stepped through into a space that she could tell at once was really big, even though it was in darkness. She could hear the wind skirling and whinnying somewhere nearby.

In the dark beside her, Stilton touched a switch. Lights came on high above, and Anna saw that she was standing in a huge hangar with enormous doors at the far end. The frame of the new airship loomed above her like the skeleton of a metal whale.

She let her eyes run over it, judging its lines, remembering other airships long ago, working out how this one would look when that frame was packed with gas-cells and covered with an envelope. In her mind she fitted on the gold-painted tail fins that she could see stacked against the wall. It was going to be a strange-looking ship, she thought. But strange in a good way; fierce and fast. It was going to be beautiful, and it had been so long since she had seen anything beautiful that tears came into her eyes.

"She is called the *Golden Arrow*," said Stilton Kael.

Anna walked all around the new ship, looking up, letting the shadows of the aluminum ribs fall across her face while Stilton watched her. She sensed that he was eager for her approval. She studied the half-built gondola. "That will catch the wind and slow her," she said. "How many will be in the crew?"

"Just two," he told her. "Me and a copilot. That is one of the rules of the Boreal Regatta, no more than two flyers to each ship."

"You need a smaller gondola, then. It doesn't need to be a house. There are ways of squeezing everything in. I can show you."

"Thank you!" said Stilton. "I'm so glad you're here! That's what I've needed, you see. Someone who really knows airships inside and out. My father lends me workers sometimes, to help assemble the larger parts of the structure, but they're just stupid thralls, they don't have your knowledge, Miss—er . . . ?"

It took her a moment to realize that he wanted to know her name. Nobody had wanted to know her name for a long time. If they wanted her, they could call her by her number, which was stamped on the iron thrall-collar around her neck.

"Fang," she said. "Anna Fang."

"Well, Miss Fang, do you know how rudder controls work? Gas lines? 'Lectrics?"

Anna had been eleven when Arkangel ate her. She remembered helping Ma and Pa with little chores aboard the *Mermaid*. She remembered climbing out on the tail fins to scrape rust off the elevator cables. She remembered the smell of *luftgaz* as the gas-cells were refilled at Airhaven docks. She had only dimly understood how those things worked; she'd just been copying what her parents did. But now she sensed an opportunity open like a golden doorway in the air between her and Stilton Kael. This was her way out of the work-gangs. She would have taken it even if she had never set foot on an airship.

She nodded.

"Excellent!" said Stilton. "I'm going to inform Kael Industries that I'm transferring you to my private service. There's a spare storeroom next door to this hangar where you can live. We'll find you some new clothes and you can get yourself, ah, cleaned up a bit . . ."

He waited for her to thank him, but she did not say anything.

"It's all right," he promised. "It won't be like the thrall-yards. I'm not like your old overseers down there. I'm different. I don't belong in Arkangel any more than you do, not really. I'm *better* than this place."

Stilton really was different. He thought of himself as a free spirit and a dreamer of great dreams. The rest of Arkangel thought of him as a fool.

His mother had come from Venice, that improbable raft resort, more a dream than a city. She had been sadly unsuited to life aboard the Hammer of the High Ice, and she had died when Stilton was only small. But a few of her soft southern notions seemed to have seeped into the boy's blood. The books she had brought to Arkangel with her had given him his love for poems. He was fascinated by the paintings that still hung in her former bedroom, like windows into a richer, finer world where beautiful women were always gazing down from battlements or sleepily accepting the love of heroes who had fought monsters and won battles just to kneel adoringly before them.

Romantic dreams of that sort had no place in Arkangel, but Stilton dreamed them anyway. Of course, the sensible, Kael part of him knew that there were no monsters to fight and that battles were dangerous and expensive and best avoided, but perhaps he could win fame and love in other ways, with his poetry, for instance—or by building a ship that could win the Boreal Regatta. He had always been good with machinery . . .

Stilton sent a note to the Kael Industries Human Resources Department, and suddenly Anna was not Thrall K-420 any more but Anna Fang, his personal mechanic. He had a bunk and two sets of good clothes brought to the storeroom next to the hangar, where she was to sleep. She was given access to a washroom nearby, where she cleaned the grease and lice out of her hair and scrubbed the filth of the salvage yards from her skin. Looking at herself there in the metal mirror was like seeing her face for the very first time. She was no longer the little girl who had vanished into Arkangel's thrall-holds.

Stilton Kael had her heavy thrall-collar removed and replaced with one so light that it was almost jewelry. Arkangel never permitted a thrall to be freed, but some thralls were trusted to mingle with free citizens in the higher parts of the city, and her new collar showed that Anna had become one of them. On errands to the air-chandlery, or in her odd free hours, she tried out the new sensation of walking alone like a free person along the busy streets and catwalks in Arkangel's Core.

"Aren't you afraid I'll run away?" she asked Stilton, while they worked on his ship.

"Of course not. Where you would run to?"

He had a point. It was winter. Arkangel was cruising the fringes of the Frost Barrens, feasting on the carcasses of towns that had died of cold. The shuttered city rang like a great bell as ice storms beat against its armor.

"You wouldn't run anyway," said Stilton. "I remember how you looked when I first brought you in here and you saw the *Golden Arrow*. People say there's no such thing as love at first sight, but there is. You want to see her finished as badly as I do."

Once the *Golden Arrow*'s skeleton was complete, Anna supervised gangs of thralls scrounged from the salvage yards while they attached the gas-cells to the inside of the frame. Then the envelope was fitted, acres of red silicon-silk dragged over the ship's ribs, tightened with coat after coat of waterproofing dope.

"It will have to be repainted," said Stilton Kael. "She is called the *Golden Arrow*, she can't be red."

"Red is a lucky color in the sky," said Anna, who was confident enough to disagree with him by then.

"Of course—I forget, you know the customs up there, the moods of the Sky Gods . . ."

"I wouldn't say that," said Anna. She had not thought about gods for a long time—the way they had let her be eaten up and enslaved by Arkangel suggested pretty forcefully that they either didn't exist, or weren't much interested in her. Now something made her pull up the sleeve of her coveralls and show Stilton the tiny blue wings inked on the inside of her wrist. "My family didn't have much to do with the main Sky Gods. We were Thursday's Children."

"Who's Thursday?"

"He was a man who turned into a god," said Anna. She remembered her mother telling her that story, and heard her own voice take on Ma's singsong delivery. "Arlo Thursday talked to the birds, and the birds showed him how to fly. Bad men tried to break his wings, so he flew away to a far land, and there he built the world's first airship as a present for a boy king."

"Then we shall dedicate the *Golden Arrow* to this Thursday," said Stilton.

"I don't know if he will help you win the race."

"He sent you to me," said Stilton, blushing as red as his airship, "so I am already in his debt."

She was hungry for parts, that little red airship (Anna was already thinking of her as she). Gas-cell valves, lightweight ladders, bolts to hold the gondola to the airframe . . . Stilton had collected a lot before he found Anna, but Anna thought she had seen better in the salvage bins. When she told him so, he sent her down to the Gut to bring it back.

It did not occur to him that the thralls down there might hate Anna, but it occurred to her. For the first few days and nights of her new life, she had thought a lot about the comrades she had left behind. They hadn't been her friends—she had been careful not to care about any of them—but it was troubling all the same, to think of them still stuck down there, living the life her luck had lifted her above. She could not ask Stilton to rescue them all, or expect his family to listen to requests for better conditions for the city's thralls: If she asked, she might end up being sent back to join them. So, since thinking about them made her feel guilty and the guilt could serve no purpose, she simply stopped.

It was unsettling to ride the elevators down into the Gut and walk among them all again. A lot of the thralls she passed didn't recognize her as K-420, in her new clothes, with two security officers walking behind her, but a few did. The scowls and muttered insults and small bits of scrap they slung at her when her guards weren't watching did not hurt as much as the desperate hope she glimpse'd in some of them. *That's K-420,* she imagined them whispering to one another as she moved through the bins where salvaged tech was sorted. *She was one of us once; maybe she'll help us.*

She found some of the things she needed in the bins and sent for an overseer to arrange their transport up to Stilton's hangar. The overseer on duty turned out to be Verna Mould. The woman kept her head bowed, eyes down, as befitted a thrall from the Gut addressing one from the Core. But once the guards stepped out of earshot, she turned to Anna with a terrible look of entreaty and said, "Can you get me up there? I was always good to you, girly. You'll put in a word for me with the masters, won't you? I'm not as young as I was, it's getting too much for me down here."

Anna looked away. "I don't care," she said. "You told me once that if I wanted to survive down here I had to stop caring about anyone but myself, and I have. You're an overseer, Verna Mould. That's the best life a thrall can hope for, aboard the Hammer."

"You've got a cold heart, you have!" shouted Verna as Anna turned away. Her voice rose to a bitter shriek that made the guards take notice. "It's nobbut an old snowball, frozen hard inside your ribs!" she yelled, while their leather truncheons knocked her to her knees.

It wasn't true, Anna told herself, as the elevator carried her back up. She *did* care. It was only that she hadn't the power to help all the thralls of Arkangel, and even if she could help a few in some small way, how did she choose which ones? An evil like Arkangel could not be fought that way, by one young woman. She wished the Anti-Traction League would come, in armored airships full of bombs and rockets, smash Arkangel to a standstill, and blast open the iron prisons of the Gut.

But all she said when she got back to Stilton was "I found the valves we need, and twenty fathoms of good cabling."

And Stilton smiled at her and said, "You're wonderful!"

Stilton had started to look at her in a strange way. He had started bringing her gifts: a warm blue jacket, then jewels and rings to show her value to all of Arkangel—you were no one in Arkangel unless you wore jewelry. He filled her storeroom home with fine furniture and a rug made from the skin of an ice-bear, a creature that Anna had thought mythical until she came in late after a long day in the hangar and stubbed her toe on its snarling head.

Even then, she could not really believe that Stilton Kael

had fallen in love with her. Sometimes in the thrall-holds she had heard other girls boasting that they were going to catch the eye of some rich man who would pluck them out of the Gut as if they were a piece of likely salvage, but she had never known it to actually happen, and she had certainly never imagined it happening to her. But here was Stilton, smiling his smiles at her, speaking all gentle, blushing as he passed her a piece of paper on which he'd written his latest poem, which began:

O Anna Fang

I feel a pang

Whene'er I look at you . . .

Anna hadn't the heart to remind him that her family name was pronounced more like *fung* than *fang*. Anyway, she thought that maybe Fang was a better name for the new Anna, the Anna who had emerged from the thrall-holds hard and sharp as a tooth.

She did not return Stilton's love. She did not think she would ever love anyone. Her heart had frozen, down there in the thrall-holds. She told Stilton so, and he said that he understood, and that he would wait, and hope, and perhaps one day she would come to love him as much as he loved her. Anna didn't think he did understand, but she said that he could wait and hope if waiting and hoping was what he felt like doing.

What else could she do? She was a thrall and he was her master. She supposed she should be glad that Stilton was treating her with such respect, but somehow she wasn't; she thought it was another sign of his weakness. The more she saw of him, the more she felt her first impression of him had been right. It wasn't just his body that was spindly and spidery; he had a spindly, spidery soul.

Still, she had to admit that Stilton was clever. His poems were truly bad, but he had a kind of genius with machines. She had known that ever since she saw him fix the engine-pods she'd found. He had worked on them with the patience of a vet doctoring a sick animal, till they were better than they had been when they were new.

Sometimes, while she watched him work, she almost liked him.

Huge tanks of lifting gas were trucked down from the air-harbor. The gasbags were inflated, one by one, until the new airship rose slowly into the air, just high enough above the hangar deck for the tail fins to be fitted and the half-finished gondola to be rolled underneath and attached. Anna busied herself with the cables that would operate the rudders and elevators. She threaded them through eyelets in the envelope fabric, ran them down into the gondola, connected them to the levers and pulleys that would operate them when the ship was in flight. The gondola bobbed gently as she moved around inside it, six feet above the hangar floor. The gasbags were not yet full, but the little airship was already yearning to fly higher.

When they tested the engines, the hangar filled with a thunder so loud that Stilton clapped his hands over his ears, but Anna liked it. It wasn't like the din of city engines. There was music in that sound, if you listened carefully enough to hear past the sheer noise of it. It was the same music that had lulled her to sleep each night when she was little, in her tiny cabin aboard the *Mermaid*.

"It will be fast, this ship," she said when the thunder faded.

"I couldn't have done it without you, Anna," Stilton
told her, looking at her in that soupy way he'd borrowed
from lovestruck knights in paintings. "When the race
begins, I want you to be my copilot."

Anna felt dizzy at the thought of leaving Arkangel. She didn't want to let herself believe that it could really happen, because she knew that the death of hope was more painful than never having hope at all. "Is that allowed?" she asked. "Even though I'm a thrall?"

"There is nothing in the rules to say that only free citizens can compete. You were born in the air, so Thursday and all the other Sky Gods will look more kindly on our flight with you aboard. And anyway, we make a good team, don't we? I was thinking that you should not just be my copilot for the race, but for all time, Anna: my copilot in life. We should marry."

"We can't," she said. "What would your family say?"

"I don't think they care what I do. I have told my father about the *Golden Arrow*, but he can't even be bothered to come down from Top Tier and look at her. Why would *he* care who I marry?" He thought a moment, then said, "At the end of the race, whether we win or lose, I shall ask the Margravine of Anchorage herself to marry us. We will come back to Arkangel as husband and wife. My family will not be able to do a thing about it."

Anna laughed with happiness then. It was not a sound she'd often made before, and it startled her as it echoed around the hangar. Stilton thought it was because of him, but it wasn't. It was just the same joy that a captive bird would feel if someone opened the door of its cage.

The Boreal Regatta was drawing near. High summer had come to the High Ice, and the sun never set. Sleek racing yachts began to arrive at Arkangel's air-harbor; the *Glory B* from London, the *Summer Lightning* from Tajikograd, the *Mossy Hare* from Dun Laoghaire.

Stilton took Anna with him to the air-harbor to see Angel Glass arrive. Angel Glass was this year's favorite; the Giaconda of the Jet Stream; the greatest racer of the age and the only woman ever to win the Transglobal Cup.

Her ship, the *Aëronette*, had the streamlined elegance of a predatory fish. When it docked, Stilton asked Anna, "Is it faster than our *Arrow*, do you think?"

She looked seriously at it for a moment and said, "No." She didn't say it just to please him; she felt that it was true. The *Aëronette* was prettier than their *Golden Arrow*, but she did not think it would be faster.

The *Golden Arrow* was almost ready. At Anna's suggestion they had rebuilt the gondola so it looked less like a flying chalet and more like a little clinker-built boat tucked snugly under the belly of the envelope. Anna sat at the controls and worked the switches that made the engine-pods rotate, the levers that angled the rudders and elevators. She longed to open the hangar doors and steer the ship out into the light of the midnight sun, but Stilton Kael said there could be no test flight. "We don't want the other entrants to get wind of what I've built," he said. "We'll move her to the main air-harbor on the morning of the race."

He was becoming paranoid as the race drew near. He had asked his father for men to guard the hangar, and when his father said none could be spared, he started making Anna change the combination on the door lock every day, and sometimes more often. He claimed that Angel Glass and some of the other aviators were desperate to get a look at the *Golden Arrow*. "'Stilton's Folly,' my family call her," he said. "But those aviators know I've got a good ship down here. I don't want them to know just how good until the race begins and she leaves them bobbing in her tailwind. Think of the looks on their faces!"

He giggled, quite unpleasantly. He was the sort of person who had been bullied at school, Anna thought. Humiliating all those rich, handsome, popular air-racers would feel like sweet revenge to him. She decided that she was going to ditch him as soon as they touched down on Anchorage. She would sign on as crew with an air-freighter, or stow away aboard a clipper. She would find her way to one of the strongholds of the Anti-Traction League. She would become a fierce warrior in their war against the cities. She would never see Stilton Kael again. She wondered if she would miss him, and decided that she wouldn't; not at all.

But she was going to miss his little airship.

*   *   *

On the eve of the race, the Direktor of Arkangel held a grand ball. Stilton Kael bought a midnight-blue dress for Anna, and she rode with him in a first-class elevator all the way to the top of the city. The windows of the Direktor's ballroom had been unshuttered, and the ice lay outside, gray as moth's wings in the nighttime dusk. Huge flues branched like the boughs of metal trees across the big room, warming the air with engine heat. Between the flues were greenhouses where trees and flowers and ferns grew. Between the greenhouses, and on the little winding paths that wandered through them, the Direktor's guests were gathered in chatty little groups, the women in gowns of every color, the men in formal robes of black and gray. Racers and their copilots strutted and preened like exotic birds blown in on the south wind. Handsome Rex Huntingtower of London, Dun Laoghaire's Niall Twombley, the Kreuzer brothers from the Dortmund Conurbation. Angel Glass was the most beautiful creature Anna had ever seen, with her braided, honey-colored hair and her long, red leather coat.

Anna followed Stilton while he went from one group to the next, laughing over-loudly at the other racers' jokes

while he waited for them to notice him. They never did. Looking up through a skylight, she saw a bird hovering in the clear air above the city. It was some sort of hawk, she thought, and it was just hanging there, sometimes making tiny adjustments to the angle of its wings and tail-feathers to keep it balanced on the wind. *I'll be free soon*, she told herself. *I'll be just like that bird. I'll fly where I please. I'll fly to the lands of the Anti-Traction League. I'll tell them what Arkangel is like, and they'll give me bombs and rockets and I'll come back and smash this place forever . . .*

"Ah, Stilton," boomed a man's voice, and the man came with it, a big, red-faced, white-bearded old man with rich embroidery all over his black robes and not a flake of kindness anywhere in his face or eyes.

"Father," said Stilton. He bowed stiffly and stepped a little farther away from Anna.

"You're still planning on entering this damned silly race in your damned silly airship, are you?"

"Yes, Father. The *Golden Arrow* is to be moved up to the air harbor first thing in the—"

"Then you'll be needing a copilot, I suppose."

"I have one," said Stilton, and waved vaguely at Anna. "This is Thrall K-420, she's . . . she helped me with the construction . . ."

Viktor Kael looked at Anna, but it seemed that thralls were made of some substance that his cold old eyes could not detect. He ignored Stilton's stumbling introductions and said, "I've just had a word with the Direktor. His eldest boy is keen to have a go at this air-racing lark." He pointed behind him at a clean, pink, overfed thug with cropped blond hair and a fancy flying jacket that had never left the ground. "There's your copilot. Rudi Masgard. Be damn good for the family brand to link ourselves with the Direktor's lad. Damn good."

Anna waited for Stilton to object. She waited for him to say, "Anna Fang is my copilot." Because all that talk of love must have meant something, mustn't it?

But Stilton just said, "Yes, Father! Thank you, Father!"

"Don't mention it," rumbled Viktor Kael. "Just make sure you bring young Masgard back in one piece. The air-trader Sheybal said he'd be interested in buying your ship after the regatta's done. We'll hold off on discussing a price, though. It'll be more valuable if it wins."

When he had moved on, Anna whispered, "But what about . . ."

"It's the Direktor's son," said Stilton. "I can't turn him down."

"I'll come anyway," said Anna fiercely. "I'll stow away. I'll make a nest for myself up between the *Arrow*'s gasbags and—"

"You can't!" said Stilton. "The weight. Every ounce counts, you know. And what if they check the ships over before we leave and find you? I'd be disqualified!"

"But we were going to . . . When we get to Anchorage, you said . . ."

"It will be all right," Stilton promised. She could feel his need to get away from her, before Rudi Masgard or his father noticed him having this urgent, whispered conversation with a thrall. Although she had never loved or even much liked him, she still felt shocked at how easily he had betrayed her.

"Wait here, K-420," he said. "I won't be gone long."

He left her there and went off to talk to Masgard. She cursed herself for being so upset. She had broken her own rule and let herself care. Not about Stilton, but about his airship. He had been right about that. She had fallen in love with that little ship the moment she saw it, and she had loved it ever since with all the love in her frozen heart . . .

She looked up at the skylight again, mainly to stop anyone seeing the tears in her eyes. The sky above the city was a deeper blue than before. The hawk had gone.

Angel Glass stood in front of a huge mirror in the ladies'
restroom, repairing the black wings of mascara that tilted
upward from the corners of her eyes. She didn't look
around when Anna came in behind her. Perhaps she
thought Anna was the attendant.

"Stilton Kael's ship is much faster than people think,"
said Anna.

That made the aviatrix look at her.

"She has reconditioned Jeunet-Carot engines and a

clever new compressor system that means she can change altitude quickly and easily without wasting gas," said Anna. "But Kael has only one thrall to help him. If his ship were to be damaged somehow, there's no way he could have her ready in time to join the race."

She took the mascara pencil from Angel Glass and wrote a number on the mirror. "That is the code that opens the access door into Kael's hangar," she said. There were little linen towels in a basket beside the sinks. She used one to wipe the mirror clean. "There will be nobody around down there now."

She threw the towel into the laundry bin and left, and Angel Glass watched her go.

It was late, and the night had grown as dark as it was likely to. An eerie dusk lay over the ice, made eerier by the Northern Lights, which had chosen that moment to put on a rare summertime display. As the green veils swayed and glimmered above Arkangel, the Direktor's guests crowded to his windows to watch, debating whether this was a good omen or a bad one. The Arkangelsk were uneasy, for they believed that on the nights when the aurora shone most brightly, the ghosts of the dead came down to dance upon the High Ice. But the aviators said that the lights were just the banners of the gods, and anyway, they would much rather the dead were having a good time on the ice than up in the sky waiting to make trouble.

Anna stood listening, watching the ghost-lights ripple like windblown curtains. She heard Stilton Kael whinny with laughter at some feeble joke his new copilot made. She heard Angel Glass tell someone, "Well, it is time I was turning in; I must get my beauty sleep before the race! Oh no, you must stay! Enjoy yourselves . . ."

Anna waited for five minutes, then followed the aviatrix out. Nobody noticed her leave.

She took a public elevator down to the second tier, and stopped in at her quarters on the way to the hangar. She took a bag and filled it with her clothes and a few bits of food she had hidden away because hiding food away was what you did when you had lived in the thrall-holds. Then she hurried through the empty corridors to the hangar.

There was no way of telling whether anyone was inside or not. As she entered the combination into the lock, Anna hoped she had not misjudged Angel Glass. But the Giaconda of the Jet Stream was already inside the hangar. She was standing under the *Golden Arrow*, looking up at its starboard engine-pod, gripping a big wrench that she had taken from one of the open toolboxes. For a moment Anna felt a cold terror that she had wasted too long packing and the sabotage had already been done. But the pod was undamaged.

She closed the door very softly behind her and typed more numbers into the keypad beside it.

Angel Glass seemed slightly surprised to see her, but she hid it well. "You were right, thrall," she said. "She *is* a good ship."

"She has the wrong name, though," said Anna. "I've never liked *Golden Arrow*."

"What would you call her?"

"My father's ship was called the *Mermaid*," said Anna. "So I thought about calling this one *Mermaid Two*. But she doesn't look like a proper mermaid. She's all made of bits

and pieces. Once, when we landed on a raft city, someone told me they had a real mermaid in the museum there and I made my ma take me to look, but it was a fake, just an old skate carved into a sort of figure, with hair glued on. Ma thought I'd be disappointed, but I thought it was clever. It was called a Jenny Haniver. So that's what I'm going to call this ship, now she's mine. My *Jenny Haniver*."

"Now she's yours?" asked Angel Glass.

"Yes. I'm stealing her. I'm going to get in and start the engines and you're going to release the mooring cables and open the hangar doors. That's why I needed you down here."

"To help a slave escape?" said Angel Glass. "I don't think so!"

"Oh dear!" said Anna. "Then I shall have to raise the alarm! Everyone will be terribly shocked that the great Angel Glass has broken into a rival's private hangar, planning to cripple his airship . . ."

"I didn't break in! You gave me the combination!"

"I don't remember doing any such thing."

"In the restrooms, upstairs, you stupid girl! You wrote it on the mirror, you said—"

"I don't remember ever speaking to you before, Miss Glass."

Angel Glass strode furiously toward her. Anna wondered just how far the other woman was prepared to go, wondered whether she was about to be attacked— but the aviatrix just dropped the wrench and keyed the number that Anna had given her earlier into the door lock.

The door did not open.

"You changed the combination!"

"It will only take a few moments, for you to open the doors and release the cables," said Anna. "You wanted the *Jenny* out of the race, didn't you? She will be. I will fly her far away."

"Is she fully fueled? Provisioned?"

"She's got fuel enough to get me away from Arkangel, and I'm used to going hungry."

The aviatrix gave an exasperated snort. She wasn't really pretty at all, thought Anna, not with that hard, angry look on her face. But she nodded, and said, "Hurry, then. Get aboard your ship, thrall."

"Shall I show you how to release the cables?"

"I know how to release mooring cables, kiddo."

Anna snatched up her bag and scrambled through the hatch, into the fresh-woodwork smell of the little airship's gondola. She turned on the cabin electrics, and the dashboard lights set green shadows in the hollows of her face. She watched Angel Glass move around the hangar releasing the mooring cables and listened to her own heart thud inside her chest. When she started the engines people were going to hear and come running, and when they found the door locked they were going to break it down. When they found her gone they would launch pursuit ships, and she couldn't be completely sure that she had enough fuel and skill to stay ahead of them. She would be alone and hunted. Her life would be measured in desperate moments. But she would be free.

So she switched on the engines, and their music drowned out the rumble of hydraulics as Angel Glass pulled the lever that opened the hangar doors. A shaft of midnight sunlight reached into the hangar and widened as the big doors slid apart. The aurora flowed across the sky outside. Angel Glass ran to the open hatchway of the gondola and said, "How do I get out? What's the new combination?"

"Your coat!" shouted Anna.

"What?"

"Your coat. It's really nice. Give me it and I'll tell you."

The aviatrix started to say something unladylike, then gave up, pulled off her long red coat, and flung it into the gondola. Anna told her the combination. "But hurry," she added. "Kael security will already be on their way!"

Angel Glass did say something unladylike then, but it was lost in the song of the engines as Anna switched them to full ahead and the ship sprang forward. She had never steered an airship from its hangar before, but she had watched her ma and pa do it many and many a time. She felt as if they were with her, standing behind her in the gondola, watching over her as she worked the controls.

The *Jenny Haniver* slipped out into the arctic twilight, rising up and away from Arkangel as fast as an airship could go, and the Gods of the Sky hung out their glowing flags to welcome her.

The Gasbag and Gondola was getting too busy for storytelling. On the low stage by the window, Patigul Akhun was tuning up her forty-string guitar, and aviators were already shouting requests to her to play the old songs they loved. A girl came pushing through the crowd, a skinny, fair-haired girl wearing the white uniform of the Traktionstadt Coblenz Luftkorps. She was part of Coma Korzienowski's crew, and when she reached the table she leaned down to whisper a quick, urgent message in her ear. Anna watched a frown appear on Coma's large, pretty face. Coma, catching her eye, shrugged, deciding that the message was not so secret, and too interesting not to share. "London is still moving east," she said. "It ate a town called Salthook in the old North Sea, and it's coming our way at high speed. I can't imagine what Lord Mayor Crome is thinking . Doesn't he know the big Panzerstadts will eat his city up?"

"Perhaps he wants it to be eaten," said Anna. "London has been in hiding for years. Perhaps its rulers have grown tired of skulking in the western hills and decided to end it all. Perhaps Crome's gone mad."

But she didn't really think that. Magnus Crome was the cleverest, most cunning Lord Mayor London had ever had, and if he was driving his city back into the Hunting Ground, he must be sure that it could defend itself against larger predators. That troubled her. It suggested that the rumors she had heard were true: Crome had some long-laid scheme he was putting into action. While the others started arguing about what London's plans might be, Anna stood up and buttoned her coat and went outside and down a ladder to the docking ring where the Jenny Haniver was moored.

TRACTION
CITY BLUES

1

These shards had been mountains once. In Ancient times they had been called the Alps. But bad things had happened to them in the centuries since: earthstorms and ice ages, a Slow Bomb strike in the Sixty Minute War. Now they were just the Shatterhorns, a steep land of rubble riven by clefts and rat-runs where the mining towns crawled.

But tonight the mining towns had fled, and the Shatterhorns shivered at the coming of a new disaster. Up from the lowlands, engines roaring, smokestacks spewing thunderheads, a city was advancing. Banks of gigantic caterpillar tracks ground granite to gravel under it. Above the tracks, stacked in seven tiers like the layers of a wedding cake, the body of the city towered; factories and work-yards fume-wrapped on the lowest level, shops and houses on the ones above. The higher tiers were smaller and had parks about their edges, though the wild winds of the Shatterhorns had stripped the trees of leaves. On the tiny topmost tier, among the council offices and politicians' palaces, an ancient temple had been rebuilt in honor of the city's past. Even the wretched Anti-Tractionists, watching from their hilltop hovels as it lumbered by, recognized the famous dome of St. Paul's Cathedral. It told them that this juggernaut was not just any moving city. This was London, first and greatest of all the Traction Cities of the earth, and it was making its way across the high passes to hunt upon the plains of Italy.

Anna Fang steered her red airship *Jenny Haniver* into the little air-harbor on the base tier. Those quays were not much used since the new harbor had opened higher up, and the only things moored there were some London scout ships with blank white envelopes like the speech

bubbles of cartoon characters with nothing left to say. The customs officials were lazy, bored, and easily bribed. They accepted Anna's story about collecting a cargo as easily as they pocketed the gold coins she slipped them.

It was a whole year since she had fled from Arkangel. The *Jenny Haniver* had carried her easily to the Spitzbergen

Static, where she had hoped to join the Anti-Traction League in its fight against the moving cities. But the Anti-Tractionists of Spitzbergen were not interested in fighting. So she had let a trapper hire the *Jenny* to carry his cargo of furs to Airhaven, and on Airhaven she had picked up another cargo, and quite quickly she had found herself a free trader on the Bird Roads.

But just being free was not enough. The farther she flew from Arkangel, the more angry she grew at what had happened to her there. The whole system of Municipal Darwinism, which made things like Arkangel possible, seemed to her a poison upon the earth. She felt that she had a duty to strike some blow against it, and if the League would not help her, then she would have to strike alone.

She walked out of the airdock and into the warren of streets that filled that part of London's Base Tier. It was busier than she had expected. Crowds of workers were spilling from the elevator stations to go on duty in the engine districts, laughing and shouting jokes at each other as they stumbled down the steeply tilted pavements. London didn't venture often onto slopes as steep as these. It was a novelty for Londoners when their streets turned into hills. Anna walked among them with her head down, her long red coat buttoned, an empty canvas shoulder bag flapping against her side. At intersections she sometimes paused to study the palm of her hand, on which she had copied the map that an air-trader in Peripatetiapolis had drawn for her. It led her from busy places into quieter ones, past Limehouse elevator station and a pub called the Sense of Doubt, and eventually down an alleyway between two massive ducts to the shop of Fatberg Slim.

F. Slim: Salvage, said the sign above the low doorway, but Fatberg's definition of salvage was a slippery one. He did buy clothes and furniture from the salvage yards when London ate a smaller town, but he had other sources, too. A box of tools or a crate of machine parts lost anywhere in the lower parts of London would find its way to Fatberg's shop. Watches and purses and tiepins and brooches that went mysteriously missing on the higher tiers turned up there, too. The place was stuffed with stuff; a maze of shelves groaning softly under the weight of all that junk and treasure, and at the center of the maze sat Fatberg himself, filling out his stained white suit the way a sausage fills its skin.

His large pink face arranged itself into a smile when Anna came through the maze to him that night. Business had been slack since the climb started; everyone was busy in the engine districts, or put off by the heat and noise that filled Base Tier. "A customer!" he said. "And such a pretty one! What can I tempt you with, little lady? I've got all sorts of trinkets here . . ." He spun on his straining swiveling chair and waved a plump hand at the glass cabinets where he kept the jewelry. "The great advantage to living in the chassis of a Traction City is that the stuff the rich folk drop on tiers above comes down to us. Maybe a lady on Tier One feels the clasp of her blast-glass necklace break while she's taking the air in Circle Park. Before she can stop it—oh, heavens! Oh, help!—it's slithered through one of the gratings in the deck! It lands in the busy streets of Bloomsbury, where the wheels of one of those newfangled electric carriages clip it and send it through another grating, down to Tier Three. And slowly, if we're lucky and no sharp-eyed bugger on the higher levels spots it, the ceaseless movements of our mighty city shake it down from level to level, through grating after grating, until it lands at last where all things must, here on Base Tier, where myself and my team of highly trained associates can gather it up and pass it on to those who are pretty enough to deserve it. For a suitable consideration, of course."

"I'm not interested in jewelry," said Anna Fang.

"Oh." Fatberg glanced at her long red coat and wondered where she'd pinched it. "What, then?"

"I was told you sell . . . equipment."

Fatberg's narrow eyes grew narrower. He leaned toward her. "Can you be more specific?"

"I want a magnetic demolition charge."

"Explosives, eh?" Fatberg rose from his chair. Anna was tall, but he towered above her. His fatness no longer looked soft; there was muscle under it. "It would be illegal for me to sell explosives. Especially to a foreigner."

"I imagine it would be very expensive," said Anna, and took out her purse.

Fatberg heard the coins clink even above the thunder of his city. He sniffed and, without looking away from Anna, said, "Ernie, fetch one of those *items* from the store cupboard."

A young man with tattoos on his face emerged from

the shadows nearby and hurried off into the deeper ones
that lay at the rear of the shop. A few moments later he
was back, carefully carrying a flat, silvery disc that looked
like a metal chocolate box or the lid of a tiny manhole.
Cities that didn't have London's vast dismantling yards
used such charges to break up small towns they caught.
Attach them to a weak point on the hull, turn that switch
to start the timer, stand well back, and *boom*. Use a few
hundred and there's no more town, just chunks of useful
scrap.

Anna placed one of the gold coins from her purse in
the sweaty center of the hand Fatberg held out. He
made the coin vanish into one of his many pockets,
watching her all the while with a look of great seriousness,
then held out his hand again. She hesitated for just a
moment, then gave him another coin. When he had
taken four, his face suddenly spread into a grin again.
"Nice doing business with you, miss. I hope you'll be
very careful what you do with this little toy, and if you
ain't, well, I don't know anything about it."

Anna could feel his eyes on her as she put the charge
into her bag and left the shop. The charge was surprisingly

heavy. She stopped at the end of the alley to set her bag down and adjust the strap. Then, instead of going back toward the airdock, she turned deeper into Base Tier, making for the district called Mortlake.

It was an old industrial section, part of a huge complex called the Wombs. Back in the golden age of Municipal Darwinism, London had built whole suburbs for itself there, refitting handy little towns it caught and sending them off covered in bunting and civic pride, carrying some of London's excess population away with them. But it was sixty years since the last suburb had been launched, and Mortlake had fallen into disuse. *Danger—Keep Out* said signs on the chain-link fences that barred all the approaches. Under the words was a toothed red wheel, the symbol of the Guild of Engineers.

Anna reached one such fence, looked left and right to check she was alone, then went over it as easily as a monkey and on into Mortlake's corroded gloom.

There were no lights here. No names above the rusty shop fronts. Posters on the huge support pillars advertised shows and patent cure-alls from fifty years before. The district's few narrow streets wound around the flanks of the colossal hangars in which suburbs had once been built. In the rare places where daylight could reach, clumps of nettles sprouted wanly among the rust flakes on the deck.

Anna took a flashlight from her pocket. The beam fingered drifts of debris that had collected against forward-facing walls as the city climbed. It poked through dark doorways, and once lit up the edges of a huge rust hole in the deck, through which Anna could see the wheels turning beneath the city.

"Hello!" she called nervously, into the immense dark of one of the old Wombs. "Collector?"

Only echoes came back to her.

She turned away and walked on, keeping the flashlight aimed at the deck ahead, afraid she might fall down another of those holes. Instead, it lit up a danger she had not foreseen: the polished toe-caps of a pair of boots.

She raised the light, and her eyes. Above the boots was a stained white suit. Inside the suit was Fatberg Slim. Behind him stood the tattooed man from his shop, and another so like him that he must be a brother, if not a twin.

Fatberg snatched the flashlight from her and turned it so it pointed in her face. "Looking for something, are we?" he asked.

"I paid you," said Anna, blinded, trying to shield her

eyes. "I paid you well. It's none of your business what I do here."

"But I think it is," said Fatberg Slim. "Don't you, lads? A stranger, a foreign stranger, wandering off into our city with a dangerous explosive item. We've got our civic duty to consider. For all we know you could be one of them Anti-Tractionist savages come to sabotage London." He held out his massive hand. "Give me the bag."

Anna cursed herself for ever dealing with him. He had her money, and now he was going to take back his merchandise. He knew she wouldn't go for help to the authorities. He would probably steal the rest of her money, too. He would probably kill her and leave her down here in the dark where no one would ever find her . . .

"Give me the bag," said Fatberg Slim again, and when she only shook her head and cowered against the rusty wall behind her, the tattoo twins stepped forward and grabbed her, dragging the bag off her shoulder.

Then something came out of the dark behind Fatberg. Big as he was, it knocked him off his feet. There was a scream. The men holding Anna's arms let go. She ran, not knowing what was happening behind her and

not wanting to know, just desperately hoping to get
away. In the dark, and her panic, she did not see the
rust hole in the deck ahead of her until she was falling
down it, into the wind beneath the city and the sudden,
shocking cold of open air.

Nets of metal mesh were strung across the gulfs between London's banks of caterpillar tracks. They were meant to save hapless workers who tumbled off the city's underside while they were repairing it. The nets were rusty, and in some places they were missing altogether, but the one that Anna landed on held like her luck. She crashed down on it and lay there half stunned. The darkness was full of the *scherlink*, *scherlink*, *scherlink* of the huge treads passing, the grumble of the wheels, the squeal and grind of massive axles. Other sounds came from above; awful screams that cut off suddenly to leave a silence that was worse. Then heavy footfalls, as if (Anna thought) one of London's statues had sprung to life and started pacing about up there.

Something dropped toward her through the rust hole, and Anna saw it falling and rolled aside just in time so that it did not crush her. It landed in the net beside her, slack and weighty, unmoving until London's movement set it swinging. It was Fatberg Slim, or had been until very recently. The dead man's left hand still gripped Anna's flashlight. By its glow she noticed that his right hand was missing, chopped off at the wrist.

London climbed higher and higher as the night drew on. Through gaps in the clouds, the people on the upper tiers could see the lakes and rivers of the lowlands glinting in moonlight far behind. Their city had never ventured to such altitudes before. They held parties to celebrate, the music of string quartets mingling with the wolf howls of the mountain wind. If London could conquer the Shatterhorns, it could do anything!

On the edge of Base Tier, snow blew in between the tier supports and melted as it settled on warm metal pavements.

It would be a quiet night, thought Sergeant Anders, as he strolled toward Airdock Green Police Station to start his shift. But then, most nights were quiet at Airdock Green. Sometimes there might be a drunk or two from the pubs on Crumb Street to deal with, sometimes a pickpocket working the crowds of engine-laborers around the elevator station on payday, but by and large there was not much crime on Base Tier to add interest to an old copper's life.

Karl Anders had been thirty years a policeman, but only three of them aboard London. Before that he had been Chief of Police on a little town called Hammershoi, just three tiers tall, that roved around the north country, right up into the Frost Barrens in the arctic summertime, stopping to trade with other towns it met. It had been a happy place, right up until that bleak February morning when it met London, hunting in the north.

Anders still missed his quaint old police station, the park on Obertier, and the wooden cupolas of the Temple of Peripatetia. But Hammershoi's engines had been just cheap gimcrack copies of the great inventions that drove London. The chase had lasted all of fifteen minutes before London's jaws closed on Hammershoi's chassis and the town was dragged into London's gut, looted and broken up to feed the hungry city.

There were far worse cities to be eaten by. At least London didn't enslave the people of the towns it ate. They were free to leave if they had anywhere to go, or welcome to stay and become Londoners, as so many had before them. So Anders stayed, using his long experience as Chief of Police to get a job with the London force. But new refugees from eaten towns weren't welcome on the higher tiers or in high-ranking jobs. He had started at the bottom again; down on Base Tier, a lowly sergeant running the quietest cop shop in the city.

He buttoned the collar of his blue uniform and pushed open the door, stepping into the hard, flickery light from the electric bulbs in their big tin shades that swung from the ceiling as the city moved. Young Constable Pym pulled himself smartly to attention and saluted when Anders came in. A keen lad, just three weeks out of school. Anders thought he might make a decent policeman in twenty years or so.

"Good evening, Pym," he said, in his careful Anglish. "Anything to report, or shall I put on the kettle?"

Pym did have something to report. He could barely keep himself from blurting it out before his sergeant had finished speaking. "Corporal Nutley's got a prisoner, sir!"

Anders put the kettle on anyway, clamping it carefully

into the special fitting on the stove that would keep it there however steeply London tilted. He struck a match and lit the gas. "What's this prisoner charged with, Pym?"

"Murder, sir!" said Corporal Nutley, coming out of the holding cell at the back of the station and locking the door behind him. "Some foreign Mossie vermin, come in at the airdock on a tramp airship, looking to blow us all up. She murdered Fatberg Slim and two of his lads! Someone heard the screaming, and we found the bodies on the edge of the Wombs. The girl—the *perpetrator*—had tried to escape by jumping down one of them rust holes what we're always telling the Engineers to patch up."

Nutley had been a policeman for as long as Anders, and he was not easy to shock, but he had seen something tonight that had shocked him badly, Anders thought. He left the kettle to boil and went over to the cell. The peephole on the door had lost its cover long ago. He peered through. A young woman sat on the bench at the back of the cell. Not really a woman, just a girl, or at that in-between stage, the age Anders's daughter would have been if she had lived. Only this girl was an easterner; amber skin, black hair, black eyes.

"She doesn't look like a murderer," he said.

"That's why the Mossies sent her, I reckon," said Nutley. "Those bozos at the customs house didn't look twice at her when she came aboard. Just a girl, they thought. But you should have seen what she did to Fatberg and his lads, Sarge. Smashed them. Slashed them. Cut off their *hands*."

"Their hands?"

"Just the right hands. All three of them. Must be a Mossie thing."

"Did you find the weapon she used?"

"Not yet . . ."

"Did you find the missing hands?"

"No, Sarge. But I found this."

He pointed to an object that lay on Anders's desk.

"A demolition charge . . ."

"That's right, Sarge. In her bag, it was. I figure she bought it off Fatberg and then lured him and his lads into the Wombs and did them in so they couldn't report her. She was probably planning to blow us all sky-high."

"With one demolition charge?" asked Anders. "And why would Fatberg Slim have reported her? He wasn't exactly a model citizen."

Nutley shrugged. "I haven't worked it all out yet, Sarge."

"Do you know the girl's name?"

Nutley picked up the arrest form he had been filling in and carefully read the name aloud, as if a good Londoner couldn't possibly keep foreign names in his memory. "Anna Fang . . ."

Anders unlocked the cell door with a key from the ring on his belt, went inside, and released the girl's handcuffs with another. She didn't speak or even move; just sat there with her skinny legs stuck out in front of her and her hands resting close together on her lap as if they were still cuffed. Pym and Nutley watched from the doorway while Anders held the demolition charge in front of her face.

"What were you planning to do with this, Anna Fang?"

The girl just stared at him. Her eyes looked older than her face. London shuddered, scrambling over boulders almost as big as itself. The bare bulb on the ceiling sloshed shadows around the cell.

Anders squatted down in front of the girl, holding the demolition charge with both hands. "It seems to me that there may be a simple explanation for all this. Did you kill

Mr. Slim and his associates? Perhaps it was self-defense. Were they threatening you? What were you planning to do with this charge?"

Anna Fang said nothing.

"If you won't talk to me, Anna," said Anders gently, "I will have to call upstairs. The Guild of Engineers is responsible for dealing with Anti-Tractionists, and they are not nice people. Once we hand you over to them, I won't be able to help you. So please talk to me."

But Anna Fang said nothing.

Anders tried not to think about the things the Guild's interrogators would do to her. He tried to think instead about how catching an Anti-Tractionist saboteur would help his career. Maybe there would be a captaincy in it for him. Maybe a better posting, up on one of the higher tiers. He left the cell, shooing Pym and Nutley ahead of him.

"Do you want me to send for the Engineers, Sarge?" asked Pym.

"All in good time," said Anders. "First, I want to take a look at where these murders took place."

Corporal Nutley had sent a salvage crew to drag the bodies
away, and the murder scene was dark and empty again.
Blood had dried in dark stains on the rusty deck. The
stains were surprisingly large. Anders shone his flashlight
on them. Around their margins, bright scratches showed
in the rust.

"What made those?"

"Boot nails, maybe."

"I've never seen anyone wearing hobnail boots on
London. The girl certainly wasn't."

"So?" Nutley said. "You're being too soft on that Mossie minx, Sarge. My old sergeant would have handed her straight over to the Engineers."

"But what if she isn't guilty?"

"She's a foreigner," said Nutley. "She must be guilty of something . . ."

"I am a foreigner myself, Corporal."

"That's different! You were eaten fair and square. That makes you a Londoner. You didn't just show up out of nowhere and invite yourself aboard and start *murdering* people . . ."

"That girl murdered no one."

"Then if she didn't, who did?"

"Quiet!" said Anders suddenly.

A few yards ahead, in the shadows beneath a huge old crane, something had moved.

"You'd best come quietly," Anders said to the shadows. "I'm armed."

Above his head big chains swung clanking, stirred by the lurching movements of the city. He went cautiously forward into the rust-scented dark and heard Nutley following. The light from their flashlights wavered over strewn ducts and rusting chunks of machinery. "I don't know why they don't just clear this district," Anders muttered. "The Council tells us to recycle everything. Why not recycle these old machines?"

"'Cos the Engineers are always talking about getting the Wombs working again," said Nutley. "Good thing if they did, too. Trouble with this city is, we don't *make* anything any more . . . Oh, flippin' 'eck!"

Anders's flashlight beam was poking down into a square pit in the deck where some other hunk of machinery had once been attached.

The pit was full of hands.

Anna Fang went to the door of her cell and looked out through the spy-hole at Constable Pym, who was crouching in front of the big wooden filing cabinet. She was not sure what to make of these London policemen. The one who had caught her as she was scrambling back up through the rust hole had been rough and angry and stupid, just as she would have expected, but she had not been prepared for Sergeant Anders's kindness. She wished now that she had talked to him. She was sorry that she had let him go off into the dark without warning him of what was hiding there.

"Here we go!" said Pym. He stood up and waved a sheaf of papers at her. He seemed to think that she would understand him if he spoke slowly and clearly. "Every week we get a copy of all the police reports from other stations on Base Tier," he said. "Corporal Nutley says there's no point reading them, but there must be some point, mustn't there, or they wouldn't send them? I knew it reminded me of something, that thing about the chopped-off hands, and here it is, listen. 'Friday tenth May. Body identified as Sidney Simmonds, Track-plate Cleaner Third Class, recovered from number fourteen axle housing. Badly mangled; right hand missing.' That's from Bermondsey. They put it down as accidental. Thought he'd got caught up in the machinery. And look, here's another, the week before, way back in Sternstacks: 'right hand missing.' And . . ."

Pym set the papers on the desk and leafed swiftly through them. "Disappearances!" he said. "Eight . . . nine . . . ten of 'em this fortnight past! Ten men gone overboard, it seems. The Guild of Engineers put out an announcement warning against drunkenness on duty. But did they fall, or was they pushed? And were they missing their right hands when they fell?"

"When I was a girl," said Anna, "Arkangel ate a little scavenger town. A nasty little place, but it didn't even bother to flee when Arkangel came swooping down on it, so it got eaten. There were thirty men aboard. All dead."

"Blimey!" whispered Pym, all saucer-eyed. "You *can* talk Anglish, then?"

"All the dead men had their right hands missing," Anna told him. "We found the hands heaped up in an old warehouse near the bows. It looked like a nest of big white spiders."

"You're just trying to frighten me," said Pym, sounding

frightened. "Spreading panic and discontent, that's what you're trying to do. Anti-Tractionists do that. I went on a course about it."

"You *should* be frightened, policeman," said Anna. "Your sergeant and the other one aren't coming back. I know what it is, that thing out there. It will kill them, too, and take their hands."

"Great Goddess!" Anders started to say, but before he could get the words out, he sensed movement in the shadows beyond the pit of hands. He swung his flashlight toward it and saw dark, oily robes, a hood with more shadows inside it, and . . . Those green lights couldn't really be two glowing eyes, could they? They must just be goggles, reflecting a green light from somewhere . . .

A raised hand sprouted knives; not one, but four. Anders heard himself shouting, "No!" Then the crash of Nutley's gun deafened him. The robed attacker stumbled but did not fall. Nutley fired again, and the robed shape went backward and then up, bounding like an ape up the side of the crane, dropping into the darkness beyond.

"After him!" Anders yelled.

They went around the crane. Robes flapped under an arch ahead and the policemen followed. Around a corner, through stacks of old crates. "He's trapped!" shouted Nutley.

The fugitive was running down a street that both men knew was a dead end. The walls of the shuttered construction hangars towered up on either side. Across the street's end stretched a wire fence, and beyond the fence was a little unmanned railway that carried solid fuel from the Gut to the old auxiliary Godshawk engines near Sternstacks. A train was passing, the streetlamps beyond flickering between the cars, and the fugitive was silhouetted against the light, slowing as he reached the fence and realized the policemen had him trapped.

"He's tall, this fellow . . ." said Anders.

The fugitive reached up with one hand and just pulled the heavy mesh of the fence apart, tearing a hole big enough for even him to climb through.

Anders kept running. The fugitive leaped aboard the last of the trucks as it trundled past. Anders ran right to the fence and stopped there to take careful aim. In all his years as a policeman he had never yet shot anyone, but this felt like a good time to start. He squeezed the trigger and the gun jumped in his hand and he knew he had hit the figure squatting on the last truck because he saw a puff of smoke or dust or something spurt from its robes. But it did not fall. It just turned and looked back at him while the train carried it into a tunnel at the base of a big metal buttress, and again Anders caught that glint of green eyes in the shadows under the ragged hood.

Nutley came running up, and they stood there side by side, winded, bracing themselves against the fence while the city lurched under them, scrambling over some granite reef.

"It's not human," said Anders.

"Not human?" Nutley started to chuckle. "What, then? A werewolf? A nightwight? Maybe we should be using silver bullets! We missed him, that's all."

"My shot hit. So did at least one of yours." Anders shook his head, staring at the curve and gleam of the narrow tracks where they plunged into that tunnel,

trying to remember where they went. "It was a Stalker,"
he said.

"They're just in stories, aren't they, Sarge?"

"Oh, Stalkers were real enough." The ghosts of long-
ago history lessons stirred in Karl Anders's memory.
There was that rusty head he used to go and look at, in
the Hammershoi Museum, when he was a lad. He said,
"There was a culture once that knew how to resurrect
the dead. Not their minds, just their bodies. Armored
them and sent them to fight in the wars they were always
having back in the days before Traction, when rival cities
worked out their differences by fighting instead of eating
one another. The last of the Stalkers were supposed to
have perished at the Battle of Three Dry Ships, but there's
always been rumors of one or two survivors. Old things.
Insane and dangerous."

"But how's one come to London?" asked Nutley.

Anders shrugged. "Up from below, I suppose. London's
been moving slow these past few weeks, creeping up
and up these Shatterhorns. A thing like that, if it was
lurking in the high places, could have climbed aboard.
Unless . . ." He turned suddenly, looking at Nutley. "It's

no coincidence. This thing appears, and that girl you arrested . . . There's a connection."

"What?"

"I don't know. Let's get back to Airdock Green and ask her."

"Sarge!" said Constable Pym excitedly, but Anders had no time to hear his news. He went straight to the cell, leaving Nutley to pour two mugs of tea fortified with a good dash of something stronger from the bottle they kept for emergencies in the top drawer of the filing cabinet.

Anna stood up as Anders opened the cell door.

"Don't pretend you don't speak Anglish," he told her. "*Everybody* speaks Anglish in the air-trade. And if you really don't we can get a translator in. But by the time I can get one here your creature may have killed again."

Anna said, "It is not *my* creature."

"It arrived the same time you did. I think maybe Corporal Nutley is right; you are some kind of saboteur and you've brought that thing aboard."

"No," she said.

"No," said Pym, from the doorway. "That's what I

was trying to tell you, Sarge. It's been here for days and days. A fortnight, maybe. There've been deaths and disappearances."

Anders looked at him, then back at the girl. Anna decided it was time to tell him the truth.

"He's right," she said. "I tracked it here. It is very old and it has been wandering the world for a long time. I followed the stories from city to city, settlement to settlement; stories of murders and missing right hands. In most of the places it's been, people don't even know what it is; they think it's a bogeyman, a hungry ghost. Aboard Murnau they called it Struwelpeter; on Manchester it's the Fingersmith. In these Alpine statics it's called the Witchfrost. Most places, people just call it the Collector. It takes the right hand of everyone it kills."

Some of the anger went out of Anders. He sat down on the cell's hard bench. "Why?"

"Maybe it's planning to open a secondhand shop."

"Very funny, Miss Fang. I meant, why did you trail it here?"

"Because I want it," said Anna. "You're right. I am an Anti-Tractionist. I hate all mobile cities. But I'm not so stupid that I think I could blow them up with little fireworks like the one Mr. Slim sold me." She shot a look of scorn at Nutley. "If I had a Stalker to do my bidding, he could tear your city apart with his iron hands. He could kill you all one by one with his steel claws."

"But why would he do your bidding?" Anders asked. "Why wouldn't he just cut your throat for you and take your pretty hand for a souvenir?" ·

The girl shrugged. "I've heard about this other Stalker, a bounty killer up in the northlands. Herr Shrike, he's called, and he kills men and women without mercy, for anyone who'll pay. But sometimes he takes pity on the young. I thought maybe the Collector would be the same. Maybe I'm young enough that he'll listen to me. Maybe I can make him turn his talents to a good cause, and help me rid the world of these juggernauts of yours."

Anders ignored the notion that destroying whole cities full of people was a good cause. "It's a hell of a risk you're taking. What if the Collector won't take pity on you?" He laughed. "Ah, but you've already thought that through, haven't you! That's why you had the demolition charge with you!"

Anna tilted her chin at him, sensing mockery. "If I clamp it to his armor and let it off, I bet not even a Stalker could withstand that.".

Anders shook his head. "Believe me, Miss Fang, if you were close enough to clamp things to its armor, you'd be dead."

"Why are we stood here listening to this Mossie minx?" asked Nutley, who had taken Constable Pym's place in the doorway. "We need to be calling for support. This thing could be halfway to Sternstacks by now, a-murderin' as it goes. Send word up top, Sarge. Get some of them lads from the Gut who think policing means posing about in fancy body armor. Let them help us deal with this thing."

"No," said Anders. "If we call for help, the Guild of Engineers will hear of it."

"Good!" said Nutley. "They got death rays and electric guns and all sorts stashed away in their Engineerium, I've heard."

"Exactly. So you can imagine how they'd love to get their hands on a working Stalker. I want to deal with this thing myself, if I can."

He left the cell door open when he went back out into the office.

"Shall I lock the prisoner up again, Sarge?" asked Pym.

"No," said Anders. "We'll need her with us. You heard what Miss Fang said. It may have a kindness for the young. We need her to lure it close, so I can pin this pretty badge on it." He held up the demolition charge, now neatly labeled as *Evidence* in Constable Pym's boyish handwriting.

"What, you mean take this Mossie cow off to Sternstacks with us?" Nutley demanded. "You're going to let her talk to that monster, and maybe turn it against us like she's wanted to all along? That's if she doesn't just run off into the dark first chance she gets!"

By way of answer to the last point, Anders handcuffed Anna's wrists together again. "If she runs, Corporal Nutley, you have my permission to shoot her. And if she can say more than ten words to this Collector fellow before I attach the charge to him, my name is not Karl Anders."

It was a long way to Sternstacks, down dingy, steeply tilted streets that skirted the central engine district, leading past the Engineers' great experimental prison at Piranesi Plaza. "That's where you're headed for," Nutley told Anna Fang with a leer. "All sorts of toys they've got in there for loosening Anti-Tractionist tongues. Literally, sometimes."

Luckily the streets were almost deserted. The only people they passed were harried engine-minders hurrying from one emergency to another, with no time to wonder where two policemen were going, or why the girl they had with them was handcuffed. They went down Shallow Street, which wasn't shallow at all that night but canted at an angle that made them shuffle and stagger like comedy drunks. At the street's end, litter sliding downhill from districts near the city's prow had collected in drifts against an old statue of Charley Shallow himself, one of London's first and worst Lord Mayors.

At Sternstacks they stepped out of the iron shadow of the tiers above into air that was cold and almost fresh. Anna looked up, hoping to see stars, but she was out of luck. All around her the huge exhaust stacks of the city rose, taller than any tower she had ever seen, some striped like garter snakes, some so fat that lesser stacks and flues twined around them like ivy around a giant tree. From their tops the smoke and smuts and filthy gas of all the city's engines spilled in clouds that blotted out the sky.

"I found a whole parasite town up there in the smog once," said Nutley. "A little flying place called Kipperhawk. They'd anchored it to London's stern with hawsers and it was hanging in the smokestream, sieving out minerals and such. Cheeky cloots."

"It's a town-eat-town world," said Anders.

They walked past darkened offices and workshops to a low, round opening where the little railway track from Mortlake emerged. A line of trucks was being unloaded there by men in the orange jackets of the fuel corps. Anders went over to the foreman. "Seen anyone come out of Mortlake tonight?"

"Mortlake?" The man looked at him as if he was crazy. "No. What's up?" He peered past Anders, trying to ogle Anna through the ripple of hot air from the engines. "Who's the girl?"

"Police business," said Anders.

"Suit yourself. But if you find my 'prentice on your travels, send him to me, would you? I haven't seen him since last tea break."

"It's here," said Anders, going back to where Nutley and the girl were waiting. "An apprentice from that fuel gang has vanished. The Collector has collected himself another hand. Where is he going, Anna?"

Anna thought about it. She thought about where she would go, if she were the Collector. "To the back, maybe. The edge of the city. He doesn't like that you saw him. He's looking for a way off."

"There are barriers all along London's stern."

"Barriers don't stop him."

They headed sternward. Walkways led aft between huge horizontal ducts. The ducts steamed, filling the air with mist. Smut drifting down from above swirled in the mist like snow gone bad. Sometimes there was actual snow as well. By the time they drew near to the high barriers at the stern, visibility was down to a few yards. When they arrived in front of an iron statue of Sooty Pete, the hunchbacked god of the engine districts, they thought for one terrifying second that they had found the Stalker. And when the strangers appeared, silently and all around them, there was no warning; their rubber-soled shoes made no sound on the deckplates, and their long white rubber coats blended perfectly with the drifting steam.

They were Engineers, with pale, bald scalps and the red cogwheel symbol of their Guild tattooed on their foreheads. There were four of them. Two carried sleek and scientific-looking guns; a third was weighed down by something vaguely gun-like but so huge, and so encrusted with wires, dials, flexes, coils, and little copper globes on long prongs, that it was hard to be sure.

"Is there a problem, Sergeant?" snapped the leader, a senior Guildsman, his eyes invisible behind faceted goggles.

Anders stepped forward, half hoping that in the Sternstacks murk these newcomers wouldn't notice Anna Fang. But they *had* noticed her, of course; the eyes of the three gunmen were creeping all over her. Anders chose his reply with care. The Guild of Engineers had started out as London's mechanics and technicians, but on a mobile city mechanics and technicians were men of great importance. Upsetting them might end a man's career.

"We are investigating some murders, sir," he said. "Three scavengers dead."

"Have you reported this, Sergeant?"

"Not yet, sir. They were Base Tier types; nothing you need concern yourself with, but it must be investigated, sir, all the same."

"And the girl?" asked the senior Engineer. His goggles glittered like flies' eyes as he turned them toward Anna.

"A witness, sir, assisting us with our inquiries."

The goggles swung back to Anders. "These dead scavengers. Had they been mutilated?"

"Their right hands had been taken off, sir."

"Mmm," said the Engineer. Behind him the man with the big gun-thing shifted position, bracing himself against its weight. The others stood still as statues (which wasn't very still on London's shuddering decks). Some of the black smut that swirled down between the stacks settled on their white coats, speckling them like dalmatians.

"You may return to your police station, Sergeant," the Engineer said. "The Guild of Engineers has this situation under control. Your witness will remain with us."

"No, sir," said Anders.

Anna looked at him in surprise.

The Engineer seemed startled, too. He raised one well-pruned eyebrow.

"She's in my custody, sir," said Anders. "For her own protection."

"You have questioned her?" asked the Engineer.

"Oh, we know about the Stalker, sir."

The Engineer did not so much as twitch a nostril, but the men behind him were not so self-possessed. Anna saw them glance at one another when he said that word.

"I didn't realize the Engineers knew about it, sir," Anders said.

"The Guild of Engineers knows everything," the Engineer snapped. "One of our survey teams encountered the creature three weeks ago, when London first entered these hills. We subdued it and brought it aboard. We have been keeping it under observation in one of the old Wombs."

"Not keeping it under very *good* observation, were you?" spluttered Nutley. "It's killed a dozen men on Base Tier!"

"That was part of the experiment," said the Engineer calmly. "We wished to see how it behaved in the mobile urban environment. London is no longer the largest or fastest city in the Great Hunting Ground. If we are to compete with the big *Traktionstadts*, we need to adjust our hunting strategies. If we could reproduce these Stalkers and insert them into the engine districts of prey cities, they might be useful. However, this Stalker has proved less controllable than we had hoped. We have lost contact with the team we put into Mortlake to study it. It has been decided to shut down the experiment."

"That contraption will stop it, will it?" asked Nutley, pointing at the big gun-thing.

"We believe so."

"You let it loose down here on purpose?" Anders said. "But it killed people!"

"They were expendable," replied the Engineer. "As are you, Sergeant. We really cannot have common policemen prying into the business of the Guild."

He stepped aside. "Shoot them all," he said. The men behind him raised their weapons. There were four of them now, not three. The one at the back, half-hidden by the smog, was very tall, and his eyes cast two green rods of light through the murk.

"The Stalker!" shouted Anna.

One Engineer shrieked as the Stalker scythed him down. The second gunman fired one shot before the Stalker killed him; the bullet ricocheted off an engine housing. The man with the giant, ungainly gun-thing pulled its triggers and it went off. Scrawling blue lightning wrapped around the robed giant like tinsel around a Quirkemas Tree. It seemed the Engineers had miscalculated, because it did not stop or even slow the

Stalker, which cut down the Engineers' leader and then turned its attention to the one who was shooting him, reaching through the lightning to wrench the big gun and its operator apart.

"Run!" said Anna, and she started to, but Anders and Nutley did not run with her. When she looked back she saw that Anders was on the ground and Nutley was stooping over him, pressing a hand to a wound in his sergeant's shoulder.

"That ricochet got him!" said Nutley, looking around at her. "Help me!"

Anna hesitated. The Stalker would kill them, she thought, and then she would be free to go back to the *Jenny* and escape into the sky. But she felt a debt to Anders; he had tried to protect her from the Engineers. Even Nutley felt like a friend now that she had seen the Stalker. She had been stupid to imagine that she could make an alliance with that creature. Human beings had to stick together against things like that.

She scurried back. Anders's face was gray. Anna did not think the wound was fatal, but the shock and pain had almost made him pass out. Together, she and Nutley dragged him behind the plinth of Sooty Pete's statue. They crouched there for a moment, united by the fear that the Stalker would come and find them there. When it did not, they cautiously stood up, peering through the clutter of beer bottles and lucky money piled around the statue's feet.

Silhouetted in the back-lit steam, the Stalker looked like a sinister shadow puppet. It was stooping over the dead Engineers, removing each right hand. Its own left hand was a nightmare gauntlet of iron and blades, but its right arm ended at the wrist in a jutting metal prong and a tangle of shredded wires. Carefully it took one of the freshly severed hands and shoved it onto the stump. The fingers jerked like a frog's legs in a school experiment. Anna imagined electricity flowing into the hand, filling it like a glove. The Stalker raised it in front of its face, into the witch-green glare of those headlamp eyes. It turned the new hand this way and that, considering, then tore it off, flung it aside, and reached for another.

"Is *that* what this is about?" whispered Anna.

How could the Stalker have heard such a faint little whisper, over all the noise of London? But it did. Its huge head swung toward Anna's hiding place. The beams of its eyes came groping for her through the vapors. It put down the hand it was trying on and came striding toward the shrine.

"It's coming!" said Nutley.

"Run!" said Anders. "Both of you, get out of here . . ."

Anna reached down and snatched her bag from him. She stepped out in front of the Stalker before Anders could tell her not to or Nutley could stop her. She held her right hand out in front of her so that the green light of the Stalker's eyes fringed her fingers.

The Stalker was moving slowly now. Perhaps the Engineers' lightning had damaged it after all. Its head seemed half-skull, half-helmet. The skull parts were still thinly papered with old skin. Everything about it was appalling.

Anna waggled her fingers at it. "Is that what you're looking for?" she asked.

The Stalker stopped in front of her, bracing itself against the rolling of the deck, its bladed hand half raised. Maybe it wasn't used to being talked to. All these years of hunting and killing and probably nobody had said anything to it more interesting than "Aaaargh!"

"Is that what this is all about?" Anna demanded again. "You lost a hand, so you're looking for another? Trying and trying and trying to find a replacement. But you

never can, can you? They're always too big or too small or too hairy or the wrong color. And so you keep on searching . . ."

The Stalker seemed confused. It twitched its head. Its eyes flickered. "Must . . . repair . . ." it said. Its teeth were metal. Its voice rasped over them like a rusty file.

"Repair?" Anna kept her right hand outstretched. The left was in her bag, fingering the smooth curve of the demolition charge. "How long have you been looking? How many hands have you tried? You need to adapt. People lose hands and arms and legs and all sorts of things, but they learn to live without them. I lost my mother and father when Arkangel ate the town we were aboard. That was worse than losing a hand or two. But I adapted, see?"

The Stalker had lost interest. "Repair," it said flatly, starting to lumber toward Anna again.

Who remembered, as she drew the charge out of her bag, that she had no idea how long the fuse was set for.

"Here," she said, holding the charge out.

The Stalker did not seem to know what the charge was. It did not seem to care. It watched Anna's hand as she reached out with the charge and clamped it to the armor beneath the Stalker's robes. Anna could guess what it was thinking. *Is this the right one at last? After all these years? Is this finally the new hand I need?* And she surprised herself with a thought of her own: *Poor old thing.*

It slashed its blades at her then, and she felt the wind of them against her throat as she sprang back and turned and ran. She glanced behind her just once. The Stalker was lumbering after her, the demolition charge pinned to its robes like a tacky brooch with one red light on it, bright as a ruby.

Then her running shadow was flung on the deckplates in front of her by a sudden, astonishing whiteness behind. Something hit her in the back and there was a lot of tumbling and bumping and the sorts of sensations that people pay good money for in fairgrounds. Time stretched out, or maybe compressed, and when it finally got a grip on itself, Anna learned that the demolition charge had not just destroyed the Stalker, it had also blown a big, roughly circular hole in the deckplate. Through this hole gravity and the steep slope of the deck were dragging her. She clawed for a grip at its raggedy edge, but there was nothing to hold on to. She hung there by her slowly slipping fingertips and looked down.

By the light that spilled past her down the hole, she could see bits of the Stalker snagged in the net beneath the city. A hand, a foot, a head with lightless eyes. The body, or whatever was left of it, was gone. Presumably that was what had torn an immense hole in the net, right under Anna's dangling feet.

Her fingertips slipped another eighth of an inch closer to the hole's edge. She said a quick prayer to Thursday, but Thursday was a god of flight, and she wasn't sure he could help with plain old falling.

Like an answer, a voice from above said, "Grab hold, Mossie!"

Nutley was looking down at her over the edge of the hole. Just as Anna's hands lost their grip entirely, he grabbed her by both wrists and heaved her up, like a Snowmad fisherman dragging his catch through an ice-hole, up out of the dark onto the hot deck, into the shouts and footsteps of approaching emergency crews.

The doctors said that Anders needed rest once they had patched him up and put his arm in a sling, but he insisted on helping Nutley escort their prisoner back to Airdock Green. "I heard what you said to the Stalker," he told her once they were there. "About your mother and father. I can see why you must hate cities."

Anna shrugged, blowing on the mug of steaming cocoa that Pym had just made for her.

"Hammershoi, the town I lived on, was pretty," said Anders, "but it wasn't well built. Some of the tier supports gave way when London ate it. My wife, Lise, and my daughter, Minna, were caught in the collapse."

"How can you serve London, if London killed your family?" asked Anna.

"London didn't set out to kill anyone. It was an accident."

"Yes, an accident caused by this stupid system!" said Anna fiercely. "This insane, evil system, this Municipal Darwinism that makes city chase city . . ."

Anders held up a hand to stop her. "It must be good to be so young, and so angry, and so certain that you're right. Me, I'm not at all sure that it was a good idea to start cities moving all those years ago. But I know there are plenty of good people aboard London, and somebody has to protect them from the bad ones. I hope you remember that, wherever you go in that airship of yours."

"I thought I was in custody," said Anna. "I thought I was your prisoner, policeman."

Anders looked at Nutley. Nutley picked up Anna's arrest report and carefully tore it in half, and then in half again. He dropped the pieces into the red recycling bin under his desk.

Anders yawned. "Goddess, but I'm tired! What about you, Nutley?"

"Same here, Sarge. Do you know, if a prisoner made a break for freedom right now, I don't think I could do a single thing about it."

"And me with this dodgy arm, I doubt I could stop her."

"But I'm here, Sarge . . ." said Pym.

"Constable Pym," said Anders, "I shall need you to type out a full report of last night's events for the Council of Guilds, taking great care not to mention any mysterious girls or disagreements with Engineers."

"But, Sarge . . ."

"In triplicate, Constable."

Pym looked helplessly at Anna, then sat down at his desk and put a sheet of paper into his typewriter. Anders leaned his chair against the wall and closed his eyes. Nutley opened a biscuit tin and peered intently into its depths. Anna went slowly to the door, opened it, and slipped out.

Ten minutes later, as she steered the *Jenny Haniver* out of the airdock into the clean west wind, she saw that London had reached the top of its climb and was beginning its descent. All the things that had slid to the back of the city on its way up would soon be sliding forward again. Far below, a new day was spreading across the foothills and the plains, lighting up lakes and rivers and fat, slow, unsuspecting towns.

Anna circled the city once, watching the *Jenny Haniver's* small shadow glide across the dome of St. Paul's Cathedral and the lawns of Circle Park. Then she flew away, east, into the rising of the sun.

The Jenny Haniver *was surfing on the edge of the night as it swept westward across the Great Hunting Ground. Anna scanned the evening haze ahead for a glimpse of London, but it was still too far west. What she could see were the lights of dozens of small towns on the move; semistatic farming platforms and small trading towns fleeing eastward as if from an oncoming storm. The* Jenny's *radio set picked up the beacons of a few larger ones that had clustered together for trade and protection. Anna altered course, homing in on the cluster. Hopefully someone there would have new information about what London's Lord Mayor was planning.*

As she descended through the dusk, she wondered what had happened to the men she had met in London all those years ago, to Anders and Nutley and Pym. Old Anders was likely dead by now, she thought, and she felt sad for him. He had been a good man and a good policeman, and he'd done more than anyone to teach Anna's younger self that not all city folk were evil.

It had taken her a little longer to work out that not everyone who lived on the good earth and called themself an Anti-Tractionist was good. She had not really learned that lesson until the mission to Pulau Pinang . . .

TEETH OF
THE SEA

Anna had decided not to murder the Sultana after all.

It was a relief. She had been working for many years as an intelligence agent for the Anti-Traction League, carrying messages and spying out information, but she had never seen herself as an assassin. Even when she planted the bomb that sank Marseilles, she had made sure to place it in a quiet part of the raft city's engine district: Marseilles had sunk in shallow water, in calm weather, and had plenty of life boats to ferry all its citizens to safety. But when the League ordered her on this mission to the island of Pulau Pinang she had sensed that she was entering new and darker territory, where she might have to do things that her conscience could not so easily excuse.

Pulau Pinang was a large, mountainous island, with white beaches round the edges and the hills green with forests, farms, and plantations of areca nut palms. It had always been friendly to the Anti-Traction League, but its Sultan had died two years previously, when his ship had been lost at sea, and his widow, who now ruled in his place, seemed to have new ideas. Instead of sending out her small navy to scare off any floating towns that tried to approach, the Sultana welcomed them, allowing them to anchor and selling them fuel and fresh water. There were rumors that she planned to turn Pinang City into a raft town and sail off to loot and burn all the other static settlements in the Hundred Islands. The High Council of the Anti-Traction League was alarmed. "We wish you to investigate," they had told Anna. "If there is any sign that she is motorizing her town, or allying herself with pirate cities, you must remove her, and we shall see that a more sensible ruler is installed."

"Remove her?" Anna had asked.

"Permanently," said the Council, and gave her a present: a red-and-gold scarf made from silicon-silk, pretty and surprisingly strong, designed for strangling Sultanas.

But even before the *Jenny Haniver* touched down Anna could see that the stories were untrue. Pinang City was not being turned into a raft; it was a sleepy harbor town just like lots of others in the Hundred Islands, with bright-painted houses lining its steep streets and crowds of children chasing the *Jenny*'s shadow toward the air-harbor. It was true that a mobile town was anchored offshore, but it was not some sinister predator city; it was a shabby little place called Dalkey, not much larger than a big ship. Little boats were clustered around it, selling fresh fruit and vegetables to the townies. A pipeline from the fuel terminal was being dragged out to it along a pontoon. If the Sultana of Pulau Pinang chose to let her people profit from trade with towns like that, Anna could not see very much harm in it.

It was early evening, and the warm air was full of cooking smells and the scent of bougainvillea blossom and the blue smell of the sea. Anna climbed the stairways between the carved fronts of old townhouses toward her meeting with the Sultana. The royal palace floated on its own reflection in the middle of a pretty water garden, tall eaves curving skyward like the wings of seabirds. Guards in lacquered leather armor watched Anna cross the stepping-stones that led to the main entrance. Girls in petal-colored dresses flitted ahead of her through the shadows in the Sultana's private quarters. She passed through a decorative cedarwood arch that must have had old-tech hidden beneath its elegant carvings, because it bleeped at her and the girls came apologetically to make her remove all the metal objects from her pockets—some coins, and a blunt penknife. The League knew about that arch, thought Anna. No one would get in to meet the Sultana carrying a knife or a gun. The girls showed no interest in her new red scarf.

The Sultana was a small, birdlike woman, neither young nor old, with an ordinary face but an extraordinary voice, very deep and beautiful. Anna liked her. They sat on the floor, facing each other across a low table while the girls served sweet drinks and little dishes of delicious food. Anna delivered the bland greetings she had brought

from the High Council in Tienjing. The Sultana was not fooled for a moment. "They think I am a traitor," she said.

"They do not think that, exactly . . ."

"But they sent you to spy on me."

Anna said nothing. She could tell that there was no point lying to the Sultana.

"The seas around Pulau Pinang are deep," said the Sultana, "but they are not that deep. There are many small islands, many hidden shoals, many hazards. The big predator towns do not come here. If little towns come, why should we not trade with them?"

The Anna Fang who had escaped from Arkangel all those years ago could have given her a hundred angry answers to that, but Anna's life in the sky had softened her; she no longer thought every town a threat, nor everyone who lived aboard a town an enemy. She said, "Then I shall pass on your good wishes to the High Council of the League, and tell them that Pulau Pinang is still their friend."

The Sultana smiled. "And now I must conclude our little talk, Miss Fang," she said. "It is sundown, and I must retire to my prayer room for a little while."

Anna went outside with her and watched her go nimbly across the stepping-stones toward a little wooden prayer room that stood on its own island in the garden lakes. It was that hour when the sky is dark but calm water still holds the light. In the trees behind the palace a nightingale was singing. *If I were going to kill her*, thought Anna, *that is where I would do it; in that prayer room, while she is alone.* And she felt glad that there was no need.

She decided to stay a little longer on Pulau Pinang. She wanted the League to know that she had been thorough. She took tea with local merchants as if she was just an air-trader looking for a cargo, and asked each one in passing what they thought of their Sultana. They had no complaints—the taxes were lower than they had been in the late Sultan's time, and the island was richer, because the visiting raft towns had brought prosperity. The Sultana was a clever woman, a much wiser ruler than her husband had been. Only one man hesitated when Anna asked him about her. He was a spice dealer named Na'a Murad, and his mild, kindly face creased into a frown when she mentioned the Sultana.

"What is it?" she asked.

"It is only gossip, Miss Fang. I should not say . . ."

"But sharing gossip is one of life's great pleasures, Mr. Murad."

"I should not say," the man repeated, but then leaned over the teahouse table and in a low voice said, "My sister's boy is a guard at the palace, and he says our Sultana has a lover. Every night she goes alone to her prayer room . . ."

"I saw it, standing among the water gardens."

"Well, there is a path from it that leads to a small gate in the outer wall, and from that gate another path descends to a quiet cove where the old Sultan sometimes liked to bathe. And up that path, on several occasions, my sister's lad says he saw a man arrive."

"Where did he come from?"

"He came from the sea. A small boat came into the cove, and a man got out and climbed the path, passed through the gate, and went to meet the Sultana in her prayer room."

"Were there no guards on the gate?"

"There were—my sister's boy was one of them—but they had orders to let this fellow through."

"And what was he like, this man?"

Na'a Murad leaned closer and his voice grew lower still. "A northerner. His face was white. Not red, like the northerners who come here on their raft towns, but truly white, like the belly of a fish. Like a ghost."

Anna laughed. "Perhaps he is a ghost? Perhaps he is the ghost of her husband, the old Sultan . . ."

"Oh no, Miss Fang. You see, the first time this man came visiting was a few days before the old Sultan was drowned."

There was only one way for raft towns to come and go from Pinang City. They left the harbor, skirted the east coast, and then took the deepwater channel that led between clustering offshore islands to the open sea. It was in that channel that the old Sultan's ship had gone down. Anna flew the *Jenny Haniver* to a little village on the coast there, just to take a look, and try to shake the odd feeling that Na'a Murad's tale had left her with. She walked on long beaches of white sand, and said a prayer at the shrine that the Sultana had built to mark the place where her husband's body washed ashore. She watched bare, brown boys stand poised like herons, up to their waists in the clear water, waiting with their fishing spears. Later she ate some of their catch, cooked on the beach over hot coals.

Around the headland from the village, something like a house stood in the surf, but it was not a house. It was part of the wooden superstructure of a raft town, holed by sea-worms and covered with barnacles. The village where the fisherboys and their families lived was partly built from such things; rusted deckplates turned into walls, the huge housing of a paddle wheel doing service as the schoolroom. The wreckage all looked fairly new. "Many towns die in the deepwater channel," the people told Anna. "Sometimes small parts of them wash up here."

Anna ran her fingers down the cut edge of a deckplate. "What tools do you use to slice them up?"

"We don't. This is how the sea sends them to us."

The offshore islands were the peaks of drowned mountains, thick with trees. In the wide passage between them the sea shone blue and innocent. "Is it storms that sink the towns?" Anna asked. "Are there hidden rocks beneath the water?"

"Bless you, lady! The sea there is deeper than anywhere else around Pulau Pinang. No shoals. No storms. The sea just takes those towns."

"Was there a storm when the Sultan's ship went down?"

"No, lady. The sea took him; that is all. The sea was hungry for his ship, so the teeth of the sea devoured it."

At dawn the next day Anna took the *Jenny Haniver* to circle the offshore islands. Clouds of colorful birds rose from the treetops as the airship buzzed by. In some of the narrow passages between the islands, rocks showed just beneath the waves, but in the deepwater channel that led to Pulau Pinang, the sea was bluest blue and only a shoal of silvery flying fish broke the surface, fleeing from some predator in the depths.

The *Jenny* flew higher, and Anna looked south across the forested uplands to Pinang City, to where the little raft town called Dalkey was steaming away from its anchorage. As it hugged the east coast, making for the deepwater passage, she steered the *Jenny* to meet it, and radioed for permission to dock.

Dalkey's mayor was called Diarmid O'Brien, a gangling, sandy man with a shy smile. Sunburned skin was peeling from his big nose and from the bald patch he revealed when he took off his straw hat to welcome Anna to the tiny airdock. "Not many air-traders stop by," he said, as if apologizing for his ramshackle little raft. "We're just a tinker town, to be fair. Started our wanderings in my granddaddy's day, way up north somewhere, and just kept going. You know how it is. Always a new thing to see, always a new horizon to peek over . . ."

"I know that feeling," Anna said. "Have you been to Pulau Pinang before?"

"First time. We passed this way a few years back, but that was in the old Sultan's time and they weren't keen on raft towns visiting back then. You?"

"Can I talk to you privately?" she said.

"Sure," said O'Brien. "Make a way for the lady there," he told the small crowd of townspeople who had gathered to gawp at the tethered airship.

Anna followed him from the airdock to his town hall. It wasn't a long way. Nothing was a long way from anything on that tiny, cluttered raft. The town hall was tiny and cluttered, too, and a small girl was sitting behind the mayor's desk. "Now then, Niamh . . ." said O'Brien, picking her up and plonking her down in a different chair. "Her mother passed away," he told Anna, "so she comes to work with me." He found another chair for Anna, dusted it, made her sit, sat down himself, tried out a couple of poses that he seemed to think made him look official and commanding, and said solemnly, "So, Miss Fang, what can we do for you?"

"You are bound for the deepwater passage?" asked Anna.

"To be sure. It's the only way in or out of Pinang City, for a raft town."

"I think it's dangerous."

"Dangerous? It was fine when we came in, Miss Fang. And didn't the Sultana herself tell me that we should leave this morning? I had a letter from her. The wind will turn against us tomorrow, she says, but today it is as calm as a pond. What makes you think it's dangerous?"

Anna started to say something, then noticed the wide eyes of the little girl watching her and stopped. What could she tell these people? *There was a shoal of flying fish?* All she had was a bad feeling. "I may be wrong," she said, "but I think you should go carefully, and be prepared to take evasive action."

"To evade what?" asked O'Brien. "Pirates?"

"I think there may be a predator town out here," Anna said.

"You've seen it?"

"No, but . . ."

O'Brien stood up. He didn't believe her story, but it wasn't every day he was visited by a pretty aviatrix and he was in no great hurry to see her fly away. "Come with me," he said. "We'll ask the lads on the bridge if they've spotted anything."

The little girl took Anna's hand as they all climbed the stairs to the top of the town hall. "I'm nearly six," she said. "I've got new shoes."

The bridge was a roomful of wheels and levers and chart tables. An old-tech machine with a glowing green screen pinged quietly to itself in a corner. A red-haired woman stood at the town's huge steering wheel, and two men with telescopes were out on a rusty balcony, scanning the sea ahead. "Nothing, Chief," they said, when O'Brien asked if they'd seen any sign of trouble. Dalkey was turning into the deepwater passage, the first of the wooded islands sliding by to starboard.

"Look here, Miss Fang," said O'Brien, leaning over the old-tech instrument. "The echo sounder says there's fifteen fathoms of water under our keel."

Anna looked at the passing islands, wondering if a predator town or a pirate fleet could be hidden under the shadow of the trees that grew right down to their shores, but she was certain she would have seen them when she flew over in the *Jenny*. Between Dalkey and the islands more fish were leaping, big ones, silver in the sun.

"There's something here," she said. "Slow your engines. Turn around."

The helmswoman glanced at O'Brien. O'Brien took the brass mouthpiece of a speaking tube off its hook on the wall and blew down it. "Engine room, all engines slow," he said.

Anna went out onto the balcony and looked at the sea. It was just as calm as before, but it was no longer such a dark blue. It was growing paler as she watched, and as she tried to work out why, she heard the pinging of the echo sounder on the bridge speed up.

She turned to look. So did O'Brien, the screen bathing his face in green light as he leaned over it. "That's not possible!" he said. "Twelve fathoms—ten—the sea floor is coming up at us!"

The sea was almost white now.

"Turn back!" ordered Anna. "Get out of here!"

O'Brien shouted down the speaking tubes again. "Full astern!" The raft town shuddered. A great swirl of roughened water widened around it as it started to reverse, and for a moment Anna thought that the disturbance all came from Dalkey's propellers. Then she realized that the stretch of sea in front of the town's bows was bulging, creamy foam streaming away in all directions as something thrust upward through the surface. One of the lookouts yelled and pointed as a dark spire broke the wave tops a hundred yards away. Another came up, and another. One rose right beside Dalkey, and Anna saw that it was a tower of dark, barnacled metal, with heavy chains and hawsers swaying from it and people scrambling up it dressed in wet, leathery suits and huge brass helmets. Beyond the raft town's prow, the last of the sea was draining from a wide, black metal deck. It seemed roughly circular, with the towers at intervals around its edges, and lower structures spaced here and there between them. Its center was sliding open to reveal the toothy gleam of well-oiled cutting gear and massive metal grabs. If Dalkey had kept to its course and speed it would have found itself sliding into that mechanical mouth, but its rapid backing had carried its stern out over the edge of the black deck. There was an awful groan of metal grinding over metal, a lurch that scattered shingles off the town hall's roof, and the raft town slid clear of the predator, crashing down in open water.

As it fled, the watchers on the town hall bridge had their first clear view of the thing they had escaped from: the immense, oily hull below the catching deck, the

towers angling inward like cranes, swinging huge grabs over the place where Dalkey should have been. The sea came off it in cataracts, almost obscuring the name someone had painted in tall red letters along its barnacled hide: *Fastitocalon*.

"What is that thing?" the helmswoman yelled.

"The teeth of the sea," said Anna. "A submarine city that preys on passing towns." She had never heard of such a thing. But why would she? Fastitocalon lived in the deep places of the sea. It only surfaced to eat a ship or the sort of small town that, if it were missed at all, would be thought to have fallen victim to bad weather or poor seamanship. Fastitocalon could have been swimming the oceans of the world for centuries, now eating a raft resort on the Coromandel Coast, now a fishing fleet on the shores of Australia, now finding its way into the deepwater channel off Pulau Pinang, which would be a good hunting ground if only the ruler of the island could be persuaded to let raft towns come there.

They would have sent a spy into Pinang City first, Anna thought. Someone like herself, who would have talked to people like Na'a Murad and discovered that the Sultana was ambitious and clever and weary of her husband. Then they would have sent a message to her. And later a boat had landed in the cove below the palace and the mayor of Fastitocalon or his ambassador had come ashore. A northerner, pale as a ghost, from spending all his life under the sea. The Sultana had met him in her prayer room, and he had promised to get rid of her husband for her if she would send a meal Fastitocalon's way from time to time. And since then he had come calling often so he could bring the Sultana her share of the loot from the towns that Fastitocalon had eaten, and she could tell him when the next one would be passing down the deepwater channel.

"We must get back to the harbor," O'Brien was saying.

Anna grabbed the helmswoman's wrist as she started to turn the wheel. "No. I think the Sultana is in league with the people aboard that thing. She'll have her soldiers open fire on you. She can't let you live, not now that you know it's down there."

"But we can't get past it," said O'Brien, "and we can't stay here! Look, it's submerging; it'll be after taking another bite at us . . ."

"We have to stop it," said Anna. "We have to fight it."

O'Brien looked incredulously at her, then back at the submerging predator. "We're going to need a bigger town . . ."

"Go into the channel between the little islands," Anna said.

"There are rocks there!" warned one of the lookouts.

"They can't do us any more damage than that monster," said O'Brien, joining the helmswoman. "If we can get through between those islands we'll reach the open sea and be away." Together they heaved the wheel, turning the town's nose toward the gap between two of the steep islands. The engines surged. Anna stooped over the echo sounder. It reported the bottom rising, but no faster than it should be. Already, she hoped, the water beneath Dalkey was too shallow for Fastitocalon to sneak underneath it for another attack. Within another two minutes they were in the narrows. Ahead, between the steep shoulders of the two islands, the open sea shone. But ridges of rock lay just beneath the surface, and when the lookouts pointed them out O'Brien ordered the engines to shut down again. Anchors were thrown out, and the town slowed to a stop, the trees brushing its hull on either side.

"At least we'll be safe here," O'Brien said.

"Question is," said the helmswoman, "how do we get out again, without being eaten by that underwater thing?"

Anna went back out onto the balcony, away from the debate. O'Brien's daughter stood there, peering between the railings at the frightened birds that wheeled above the trees. "Is that town going to eat us?" she asked.

"No," said Anna, wondering what Fastitocalon did with the people of the towns and ships it ate. There wasn't much room on it for new citizens, and who would want to live down there anyway? Maybe it sold them to a big slave market. Maybe it just drowned them.

She tried to put herself in the mind of the predator's mayor. What would he be thinking, now that her prey had escaped? What would he be doing? Fastitocalon had to keep its secret; he could not risk Dalkey getting away to spread word of it to other towns. If Dalkey couldn't be winkled out of its hiding place between the islands, he would send people to take and burn it. And that would be best done at night.

Anna checked the sun. She estimated that they had about three hours before nightfall. She let her eyes wander over the rooftops of Dalkey, spread out below the town hall's balcony like a street map. Homes, temples, boathouses, the *Jenny* on her docking pan, a couple of rusting ships in wet docks. All the way from the north this little town had come. It must have dealt with predators before.

She went back inside, the little girl trailing behind her. O'Brien and the others were arguing about how much stuff they would have to throw overboard to float the town over the reefs at high tide. She cut across them. "Do you have weapons? Heavy guns? Shells?"

"Only a half dozen cannon," said O'Brien. "They fire roundshot or grape. There's a rack of depth charges we bought when we were cruising off the mouth of the Amazon, in case of piranha-submarines . . ."

"Where are they?" said Anna.

"Locked up in the armory, but they'll not pierce the hull of that predator . . ."

"Maybe they won't have to," Anna said. "Get them

ready, and lend me a few men to help me fetch some things from the *Jenny Haniver*. And open one of your oil tanks. I want it to look as if we're damaged . . ."

In the deepwater channel Fastitocalon waited, hanging a hundred feet below the surface, ready to attack again as soon as its prey came out of that cleft between the islands. In the dim, red light of its command chamber, its mayor put his face to the eyepiece of a periscope that poked up through the town's hull to give him a view of the water above. A black cloud hung there. Engine oil, seeping from the prey's tanks. "We have damaged it," he told his officers. "When night comes we'll land boarding parties, take it the old-fashioned way."

But before night came, something else emerged from the narrow channel. The black spearhead of a ship's hull, carefully skirting the oil slick and turning toward the open sea. The mayor smiled. He had seen this before; poor fools abandoning a damaged town, thinking that Fastitocalon would not bother to eat something as small as a ship. But he knew that ship would be carrying all the valuables they could salvage in one snack-sized portion.

Bells rang, sirens wailed. The people of Fastitocalon hurried along its tubular streets to their positions as it rose from the water for the second time that day. This time it came up faster; this time its prey did not escape. As the sea spilled off the catching deck, the captured ship tipped over on its side like a toy boat in an emptying bathtub. The trapdoors opened, dropping it into the demolition hold, then closed again so that Fastitocalon could submerge.

There was no need for machinery to tackle a prize as small as this. Eager salvage men poured through the bulkhead doors and ran to where the ship lay, swords and cudgels ready to deal with its crew.

But to their surprise, there was no crew. There were no valuables, either. All that the old trawler contained was a crate full of big, cylindrical bombs the size of beer kegs, and six small rockets from the *Jenny Haniver*'s missile racks. They were all lashed together and tangled up in a nest of wires, and right in the middle of the tangle was

a timer, ticking down. But by the time the salvagemen found that, it was already too late.

Anna was standing beside O'Brien among the smokestacks at Dalkey's stern. They watched the sea in the deepwater channel heave upward and turn for a moment into a tower that, collapsing, sent salt spray blowing into their faces.

After a while a few bodies and pieces of debris bobbed to the surface.

"Is it gone?" asked O'Brien.

"We hurt it, for sure," said Anna. "I don't know if the blast was big enough to destroy it."

"Sure it was! It'll be blown to tatters!"

"Maybe. Or maybe they're still alive down there, making repairs. You'd better leave quickly, while they're busy."

O'Brien looked hopefully at her. "Will you stay with us a while? We can give you a lift to the next island."

"I don't need a lift—I can fly."

"Ah, but an airship needs a base to call home, doesn't she? You can stay aboard Dalkey as long as you like, come and go as you please."

Anna was tempted for a moment, she really was. But only for a moment. Before she went to start the *Jenny*'s engines she kissed his stubbly, sunburned cheek and said, "You get on your way, Mr. O'Brien. I have to get back to Pinang City. I have a Sultana to strangle."

Anna set the Jenny Haniver *down on the largest town in the trading cluster, a place called Stayns. It was late by then, but the aviator's café near the docking pans was still open. A canvas awning sullenly flapped its gaudy stripes in the light of some hurricane lamps. An old man snored in a chair. Two merchants were discussing the next day's slave auction, but they went quiet when Anna arrived, and left soon afterward. Perhaps they knew who she was. Perhaps they had heard how she felt about slave traders. She went to the bar, sat down on a wooden stool there, bought a drink. The barman combed his* drooping moustache with his fingers while she asked him if he had any news of London, but he could tell her no more than she already knew.

She was getting ready to go in search of someone else to ask when the children arrived. Not really children—they wouldn't think of themselves as children—but they looked like children to Anna. They were about the age that she had been when she escaped Arkangel. The girl was half-feral, an out-country scarecrow with filthy red hair, her face ruined by a

deep, ragged old scar that had healed so badly it hurt to look at it. She was trying to act as if she belonged in this place and knew where she was going, but she had a wound on one leg and she couldn't hide her fear or weariness. The boy wasn't even trying. He caught Anna watching him as he went to the bar and looked nervously away.

It's no business of yours, Anna, she told herself. Whatever their story is, whoever they're running from, you don't need to get involved. But she was already checking the pistol hidden in her boot-top, the Nuevo Mayan Battle Frisbee folded in its secret pocket on her sleeve.

"I'm looking for a ship," the boy said. "Me and my friend have to get back to London, and we have to leave tonight." That settled it: He was from London and, judging by his accent, from the upper tiers. She could help him and his friend and perhaps learn something about the city's plans into the bargain.

The boy did not hear Anna as she slid from her stool and padded silently up behind him, but the girl, sharper, turned her ruined face and stared.

Anna said, "Perhaps I may be of help . . . ?"

She'd had enough of old stories. Here was the beginning of a new one.

ACKNOWLEDGMENTS

Many thanks to Sam Smith and Peter Matthews for editing these stories, to the writer and actor Na'a Murad for letting me borrow his name, to Jamie Gregory for the design and layout, and, of course, to Ian McQue, for all the wonderful pictures.

ABOUT THE AUTHOR

Philip Reeve lives in Dartmoor, England, with his wife and son. His first novel, *Mortal Engines*, was published in the UK in 2001. Three sequels followed, the last of which, *A Darkling Plain*, won both the Guardian Children's Fiction Prize and the Los Angeles Times Book Award. Philip later wrote three prequels to the Mortal Engines Quartet—*Fever Crumb*, *A Web of Air*, and *Scrivener's Moon*. He has also written a novel set in dark age Britain called *Here Lies Arthur*, which won the Carnegie Medal, a stand-alone novel for younger readers called *No Such Thing as Dragons,* as well as an illustrated younger fiction series with illustrator Sarah McIntyre, and a young-adult trilogy, RailHead. He is also the coauthor, with Brian Mitchell, of a stage musical, *The Ministry of Biscuits*. His most recent book, *Night Flights*, returns to the world of Mortal Engines with three short stories about the character Anna Fang.

Turn the page to read the first chapter of

MORTAL ENGINES

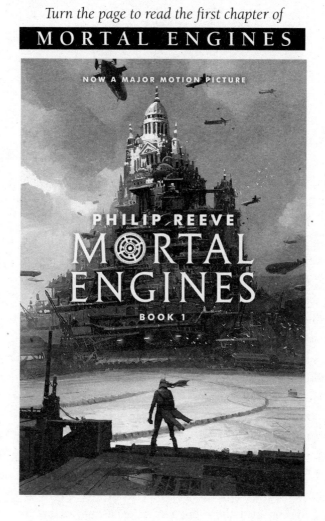

1

THE HUNTING GROUND

It was a dark, blustery afternoon in spring, and the city of London was chasing a small mining town across the dried-out bed of the old North Sea.

In happier times, London would never have bothered with such feeble prey. The great Traction City had once spent its days hunting far bigger towns than this, ranging north as far as the edges of the Ice Waste and south to the shores of the Mediterranean. But lately prey of any kind had started to grow scarce, and some of the larger cities had begun to look hungrily at London. For ten years now it had been hiding from them, skulking in a damp, mountainous western district that the Guild of Historians said had once been the island of Britain. For ten years it had eaten nothing but tiny farming towns and static settlements in those wet hills. Now, at last, the Lord Mayor had decided that the time was right to take his city back over the land bridge into the Great Hunting Ground.

It was barely halfway across when the lookouts on the high watchtowers spied the mining town, gnawing at the salt flats twenty miles ahead. To the people of London it seemed like a sign from the gods, and even the Lord Mayor (who didn't believe in gods or signs) thought it was a good beginning to the journey east, and issued the order to give chase.

The mining town saw the danger and turned tail, but already the huge caterpillar tracks under London were starting to roll faster and faster. Soon the city was lumbering in pursuit, a moving mountain of metal that rose in seven tiers like the layers of a wedding cake, the lower levels wreathed in engine smoke, the villas of the rich gleaming white on the higher decks, and above it all the cross on top of St. Paul's Cathedral glinting gold, two thousand feet above the ruined earth.

❋

Tom was cleaning the exhibits in the London Museum's Natural History section when it started. He felt the telltale tremor in the metal floor, and looked up to find the model whales and dolphins that hung from the gallery roof swinging on their cables with soft creaking sounds.

He wasn't alarmed. He had lived in London for all of his fifteen years, and he was used to its movements. He knew that the city was changing course and putting on speed. A prickle of excitement ran through him, the ancient thrill of the hunt that all Londoners shared. There must be prey in sight! Dropping his brushes and dusters he pressed his hand to the wall, sensing the vibrations that came rippling up from the huge engine rooms down in the Gut. Yes, there it was — the deep throb of the auxiliary motors cutting in, *boom, boom, boom*, like a big drum beating inside his bones.

The door at the far end of the gallery slammed open and Chudleigh Pomeroy came storming in, his toupee askew and his round face red with indignation. "What in the name of Quirke . . . ?" he blustered, gawping at the gyrating whales and the stuffed birds jigging and twitching in their cases as if they were shaking off their long captivity and getting ready to take wing again. "Apprentice Natsworthy! What's going on here?"

"It's a chase, sir," said Tom, wondering how the Deputy Head of the Guild of Historians had managed to live aboard London for so long and still not recognize its heartbeat. "It must be something good," he explained. "They've brought all the auxiliaries on line. That hasn't happened for ages. Maybe London's luck has turned!"

"Pah!" snorted Pomeroy, wincing as the glass in the display cases started to whine and shiver in sympathy with the beat of the engines. Above his head the biggest of the models — a thing called a blue whale that had become extinct thousands of years ago — was jerking back and forth on its hawsers like a plank-swing. "That's as may be, Natsworthy," he said. "I just wish the Guild of Engineers would fit some decent shock absorbers in this building. Some of these specimens are very delicate. It won't do. It won't do at all." He tugged a spotted handkerchief out of the folds of his long black robes and dabbed his face with it.

"Please, sir," asked Tom, "could I run down to the observation platforms and watch the chase, just for half an hour? It's been years since there was a really good one. . . ."

Pomeroy looked shocked. "Certainly not, Apprentice! Look at all the dust that this wretched chase is shaking down! All the exhibits will have to be cleaned again and checked for damage."

"Oh, but that's not fair!" cried Tom. "I've just dusted this whole gallery!"

He knew at once that he had made a mistake. Old Chudleigh Pomeroy wasn't bad, as Guildsmen went, but he didn't like being answered back by a mere Third Class Apprentice. He drew himself up to his full height (which was only slightly more than his full width) and frowned so sternly that his Guild-mark almost vanished between his bushy eyebrows. "Life isn't fair, Natsworthy," he boomed. "Any more cheek from you and you'll be on Gut-duty as soon as this chase is over!"

Of all the horrible chores a Third Class Apprentice had to perform, Gut-duty was the one Tom hated most. He quickly shut up, staring meekly down at the beautifully buffed toes of the Chief Curator's boots.

"You were told to work in this department until seven o'clock, and you will work until seven o'clock," Pomeroy went on. "Meanwhile, I shall consult the other curators about this dreadful, dreadful shaking. . . ."

He hurried off, still muttering. Tom watched him go, then picked up his gear and went miserably back to work. Usually he didn't mind cleaning, especially not in this gallery, with its amiable, moth-eaten animals and the Blue Whale smiling its big blue smile. If he grew bored, he simply took refuge in a daydream in which he was a hero who rescued beautiful girls from air-pirates, saved London from the Anti-Traction League, and lived happily ever after. But how could he daydream, with the rest of the city enjoying the first proper chase for ages?

He waited for twenty minutes, but Chudleigh Pomeroy did not return. There was nobody else about. It was a Wednesday, which meant the Museum was closed to the public, and most of the senior Guildsmen and First and Second Class Apprentices would be having the day off. What harm could it do if he slipped outside for ten minutes, just to see what was happening? He hid his bag of cleaning stuff behind a handy yak and hurried through the shadows of dancing dolphins to the door.

Out in the corridor all the argon lamps were dancing, too, spilling their light up the metal walls. Two black-robed Guildsmen hurried past, and Tom heard the reedy voice of old Dr. Arkengarth whine, "Vibrations! Vibrations! It's playing merry hell with my twenty-fifth century ceramics. . . ." He waited until they had vanished around a bend in the corridor, then slipped quickly out and down the nearest stairway. He cut through the Twenty-First Century gallery, past the big plastic statues of Pluto and Mickey, animal-headed gods of lost America. He ran across the main hall and down galleries full of things that had somehow survived through all the millennia since the Ancients destroyed themselves in that terrible flurry of orbit-to-earth atomics and tailored-virus bombs called the Sixty Minute War. Two minutes later he slipped out through a side entrance into the noise and bustle of Tottenham Court Road.

The London Museum stood at the very hub of Tier Two, in a busy district called Bloomsbury, and the underbelly of Tier One hung like a rusty sky a few feet above the rooftops. Tom didn't worry about being spotted as he pushed his way along the dark, crowded street toward the public Goggle-screen outside the Tottenham Court Road elevator station. Joining the crowd in front of it he had his first glimpse of the distant prey: a watery, blue-gray blur captured by cameras down on Tier Six. "*The town is called Salthook,*" boomed the voice of the announcer. "*A mining platform of nine hundred inhabitants. She is currently moving at eighty* miles per hour, heading due east, but the Guild of Navigators predicts London will catch her before sundown. There are sure to be many more towns awaiting us beyond the land bridge: clear proof of just how wise our beloved Lord Mayor was when he decided to bring London east again. . . ."

Tom had never felt his city move at such an astonishing speed, and he longed to be down at the observation deck, feeling the wind on his face. He was probably already in trouble with Mr. Pomeroy. What difference could it make if he stole a few more minutes?

He set off at a run, and soon reached Bloomsbury Park, out in the open air on the tier's brim. It had been a proper park once, with trees and duck ponds, but because of the recent shortage of prey it had been given over to food production and its lawns grubbed up to make way for cabbage plots and algae-pans. The observation platforms were still there, though, raised balconies jutting out from the edge of the tier, where Londoners could go to watch the passing view. Tom hurried toward the nearest. An even bigger crowd had gathered there, including quite a few people in the black of the Historians' Guild, and Tom tried to look inconspicuous as he pushed his way through to the front and peered over the railings. Salthook was only five miles ahead, traveling flat out with black smoke spewing from its exhaust stacks.

"Natsworthy!" called a braying voice, and his heart sank. He looked around and found that he was standing next to Melliphant, a burly First Class Apprentice, who grinned at him and said, "Isn't it wonderful? A fat little salt-mining platform, with C20 land-engines! Just what London needs!"

Herbert Melliphant was the worst sort of bully, the sort who didn't just hit you and stick your head down the lavatory, but made it his business to find out all your secrets and the things that upset you most and taunt you with them. He enjoyed picking on Tom, who was small and shy and had no friends to stick up for him — and Tom could not get back at him, because Melliphant's family had paid to make him a First Class Apprentice, while Tom, who had no family, was a mere Third. He knew Melliphant was only bothering to talk to him because he was hoping to impress a pretty young Historian named Clytie Potts, who was standing just behind. Tom nodded and turned his back, concentrating on the chase.

"Look!" shouted Clytie Potts.

The gap between London and its prey was narrowing fast, and a dark shape had lifted clear of Salthook. Soon there was another and another. Airships! The crowds on London's observation platforms cheered, and Melliphant said, "Ah, air-merchants. They know the town is doomed, you see, so they are making sure they get away before we eat it. If they don't, we can claim their cargoes along with everything else aboard!"

Tom was glad to see that Clytie Potts looked thoroughly bored by Melliphant: She was a year above him and must already know this stuff, because she had passed her Guild exams and had the Historian's mark tattooed on her forehead. "Look!" she said again, catching Tom's glance and grinning. "Oh, look at them go! Aren't they beautiful!"

Tom pushed his untidy hair out of his eyes and watched as the airships rose up and up and vanished into the slate-gray clouds. For a moment he found himself longing to go with them, up into the sunlight. If only his poor parents had not left him to the care of the Guild, to be trained as a Historian! He wished he could be cabin boy aboard a sky-clipper and see all the cities of the world: Puerto Angeles adrift on the blue Pacific and Arkangel skating on iron runners across the frozen northern seas, the great ziggurat-towns of the Nuevo-Mayans and the unmoving strongholds of the Anti-Traction League . . .

But that was just a daydream, better saved for some dull Museum afternoon. A fresh outbreak of cheering warned him that the chase was nearing its end, and he forgot the airships and turned his attention back to Salthook.

The little town was so close that he could see the antlike shapes of people running about on its upper tiers. How frightened they must be, with London bearing down on them and nowhere to hide! But he knew he mustn't feel sorry for them: It was natural that cities ate towns, just as the towns ate smaller towns, and smaller towns snapped up the miserable static settlements. That was Municipal Darwinism, and it was the way the world had worked for a thousand years, ever since the great engineer Nikolas Quirke had turned London into the first Traction City.

"London! London!" Tom shouted, adding his voice to the cheers and shouts of everybody else on the platform, and a moment later they were rewarded by the sight of one of Salthook's wheels breaking loose. The town slewed to a halt, smokestacks snapping off and crashing down into the panicked streets, and then London's lower tiers blocked it from view and Tom felt the deckplates shiver as the city's huge hydraulic Jaws came slamming shut.

There was frantic cheering from observation platforms all over the city. Loudspeakers on the tier-support pillars started to play "London Pride," and somebody Tom had never even seen before hugged him tight and shouted in his ear, "A catch! A catch!" He didn't mind; at that moment he loved everybody on the platform, even Melliphant. "A catch!" he yelled back, struggling free, and felt the deckplates trembling again. Somewhere below him the city's great steel teeth were gripping Salthook, lifting it and dragging it backward into the Gut.

". . . and perhaps Apprentice Natsworthy would like to come as well," Clytie Potts was saying. Tom had no idea what she was talking about, but as he turned she touched his arm and smiled. "There'll be celebrations in Kensington Gardens tonight," she explained. "Dancing and fireworks! Do you want to come?"

People didn't usually invite Third Class Apprentices to parties — especially not people as pretty and popular as Clytie — and Tom wondered at first if she was making fun of him. But Melliphant obviously didn't think so, for he tugged her away and said, "We don't want Natsworthy's sort there."

"Why not?" asked the girl.

"Well, you know," huffed Melliphant, his square face turning almost as red as Mr. Pomeroy's. "He's just a Third. A skivvy. He'll never get his Guild-mark. He'll just end up as a curator's assistant. Won't you, Natsworthy?" he asked, leering at Tom. "It's a pity your dad didn't leave you enough money for a *proper* apprenticeship. . . ."

"That's none of your business!" shouted Tom angrily. His elation at the catch had evaporated and he was on edge again, wondering what punishments would be in store when Pomeroy found out that he had sneaked away. He was in no mood for Melliphant's taunts.

"Still, that's what comes of living in a slum on the lower tiers,

I suppose," smirked Melliphant, turning back to Clytie Potts. "Natsworthy's mum and dad lived down on Four, see, and when the Big Tilt happened they both got squashed flat as a couple of raspberry pancakes: *splat!*"

Tom didn't mean to hit him; it just happened. Before he knew what he was doing his hand had curled into a tight fist and he lashed out. "Ow!" wailed Melliphant, so startled that he fell over backward. Someone cheered, and Clytie stifled a giggle. Tom just stood staring at his trembling fist and wondering how he had done it.

But Melliphant was much bigger and tougher than Tom, and he was already back on his feet. Clytie tried to restrain him, but some other Historians were cheering him on and a group of boys in the green tunics of Apprentice Navigators clustered close behind and chanted, "Fight! Fight! Fight!"

Tom knew he stood no more chance against Melliphant than Salthook had stood against London. He took a step backward, but the crowd was hemming him in. Then Melliphant's fist hit him on the side of the face and Melliphant's knee crashed up hard between his legs and he was bent double and stumbling away with his eyes full of tears. Something as big and softly yielding as a sofa stood in his way, and as he rammed his head against it, it said, "Ooof!"

He looked up into a round, red, bushy-eyebrowed face under an unconvincing wig; a face that grew even redder when it recognized him.

"Natsworthy!" boomed Chudleigh Pomeroy. "What in Quirke's name do you think you're playing at?"

EXPLORE THE WORLD OF
MORTAL ENGINES!

THE ORIGINAL SERIES!

THE PREQUEL SERIES!